SIGHT UNSEEN

UNSEEN

BY MARY ROBERTS RINEHART

D1534087

I

The rather extraordinary story revealed by the experiments of the Neighborhood Club have been until now a matter only of private record. But it seems to me, as an active participant in the investigations, that they should be given to the public; not so much for what they will add to the existing data on psychical research, for from that angle they were not unusual, but as yet another exploration into that still uncharted territory, the human mind.

The psycho-analysts have taught us something about the individual mind. They have their own patter, of complexes and primal instincts, of the unconscious, which is a sort of bonded warehouse from which we clandestinely withdraw our stored thoughts and impressions. They lay to this unconscious mind of ours all phenomena that cannot otherwise be labeled, and ascribe such demonstrations of power as cannot thus be explained to trickery, to black silk threads and folding rods, to slates with false sides and a medium with chalk on his finger nail.

In other words, they give us subjective mind but never objective mind. They take the mind and its reactions on itself and on the body. But what about objective mind? Does it make its only outward manifestations through speech and action? Can we ignore the effect of mind on mind, when there are present none of the ordinary media of communication? I think not.

In making the following statement concerning our part in the strange case of Arthur Wells, a certain allowance must be made for our ignorance of so-called psychic phenomena, and also for the fact that since that time, just before the war, great advances have been made in scientific methods of investigation. For instance, we did not place Miss Jeremy's chair on a scale, to measure for any loss of weight. Also the theory of rods of invisible matter emanating from the medium's body, to move bodies at a distance from her, had only been evolved; and none of the methods for calculation of leverages and strains had been formulated, so far as I know.

To be frank, I am quite convinced that, even had we known of these so-called explanations, which in reality explain nothing, we would have ignored them as we became involved in the dramatic movement of the revelations and the personal experiences which grew out of them. I confess that following the night after the first seance any observations of mine would have been of no scientific value whatever, and I believe I can speak for the others also.

Of the medium herself I can only say that we have never questioned her integrity. The physical phenomena occurred before she went into trance, and during that time her forearms were rigid. During the deep trance, with which this unusual record deals, she spoke in her own voice, but in a querulous tone, and Sperry's examination of her pulse showed that it went from eighty normal to a hundred and twenty and very feeble.

With this preface I come to the death of Arthur Wells, our acquaintance and neighbor, and the investigation into that death by a group of six earnest people who call themselves the Neighborhood Club.

The Neighborhood Club was organized in my house. It was too small really to be called a club, but women have a way these days of conferring a titular dignity on their activities, and it is not so bad, after all. The Neighborhood Club it really was, composed of four of our neighbors, my wife, and myself.

We had drifted into the habit of dining together on Monday evenings at the different houses. There were Herbert Robinson and his sister Alice—not a young woman, but clever, alert, and very alive; Sperry, the well-known heart specialist, a bachelor still in spite of much feminine activity; and there was old Mrs. Dane, hopelessly crippled as to the knees with rheumatism, but one of those glowing and kindly souls that have a way of being a neighborhood nucleus. It was around her that we first gathered, with an idea of forming for her certain contact points with the active life from which she was otherwise cut off. But she gave us, I am sure, more than we brought her, and, as will be seen later, her shrewdness was an important element in solving our mystery.

In addition to these four there were my wife and myself.

It had been our policy to take up different subjects for these neighborhood dinners. Sperry was a reformer in his way, and on his nights we generally took up civic questions. He was particularly interested in the responsibility of the state to the sick poor. My wife and I had "political" evenings. Not really politics, except in their relation to life. I am a lawyer by profession, and dabble a bit in city government. The Robinsons had literature.

Don't misunderstand me. We had no papers, no set programs. On the Robinson evenings we discussed editorials and current periodicals, as well as the new books and plays. We were frequently acrimonious, I fear, but our small wrangles ended with the evening. Robinson was the literary editor of a paper, and his sister read for a large publishing house.

Mrs. Dane was a free-lance. "Give me that privilege," she begged. "At least, until you find my evenings dull. It gives me, during all the week before you come, a sort of thrilling feeling that the world is mine to choose from." The result was never dull. She led us all the way from moving-pictures to modern dress. She led us even further, as you will see.

On consulting my note-book I find that the first evening which directly concerns the Arthur Wells case was Monday, November the second, of last year.

It was a curious day, to begin with. There come days, now and then, that bring with them a strange sort of mental excitement. I have never analyzed them. With me on this occasion it took the form of nervous irritability, and something of apprehension. My wife, I remember, complained of headache, and one of the stenographers had a fainting attack.

I have often wondered for how much of what happened to Arthur Wells the day was responsible. There are days when the world is a place for love and play and laughter. And then there are sinister days, when the earth is a hideous place, when even the thought of immortality is unbearable, and life itself a burden; when all that is riotous and unlawful comes forth and bares itself to the light.

This was such a day.

I am fond of my friends, but I found no pleasure in the thought of meeting them that evening. I remembered the odious squeak in the wheels of Mrs. Dane's chair. I resented the way Sperry would clear his throat. I read in the morning paper Herbert Robinson's review of a book I had liked, and disagreed with him. Disagreed violently. I wanted to call him on the telephone and tell him that he was a fool. I felt old, although I am only fifty-three, old and bitter, and tired.

With the fall of twilight, things changed somewhat. I was more passive. Wretchedness encompassed me, but I was not wretched. There was violence in the air, but I was not violent. And with a bath and my dinner clothes I put away the horrors of the day.

My wife was better, but the cook had given notice.

"There has been quarreling among the servants all day," my wife said. "I wish I could go and live on a desert island."

We have no children, and my wife, for lack of other interests, finds her housekeeping an engrossing and serious matter. She is in the habit of bringing her domestic difficulties to me when I reach home in the evenings, a habit which sometimes renders me unjustly indignant. Most unjustly, for she has borne with me for thirty years and is known throughout the entire neighborhood as a perfect housekeeper. I can close my eyes and find any desired article in my bedroom at any time.

We passed the Wellses' house on our way to Mrs. Dane's that night, and my wife commented on the dark condition of the lower floor.

"Even if they are going out," she said, "it would add to the appearance of the street to leave a light or two burning. But some people have no public feeling."

I made no comment, I believe. The Wellses were a young couple, with children, and had been known to observe that they considered the neighborhood "stodgy." And we had retaliated, I regret to say, in kind, but not with any real unkindness, by regarding them as interlopers. They drove too many cars, and drove them too fast; they kept a governess and didn't see enough of their children; and their English butler made our neat maids look commonplace.

There is generally, in every old neighborhood, some one house on which is fixed, so to speak, the community gaze, and in our case it was on the Arthur Wellses'. It was a curious, not unfriendly staring, much I daresay like that of the old robin who sees two young wild canaries building near her.

We passed the house, and went on to Mrs. Dane's.

She had given us no inkling of what we were to have that night, and my wife conjectured a conjurer! She gave me rather a triumphant smile when we were received in the library and the doors into the drawing-room were seen to be tightly closed.

We were early, as my wife is a punctual person, and soon after our arrival Sperry came. Mrs. Dane was in her chair as usual, with her companion in attendance, and when she heard Sperry's voice outside she excused herself and was wheeled out to him, and together we heard them go into the drawing-room. When the Robinsons arrived she and Sperry reappeared, and we waited for her customary announcement of the evening's program. When none came, even during the meal, I confess that my curiosity was almost painful.

I think, looking back, that it was Sperry who turned the talk to the supernatural, and that, to the accompaniment of considerable gibing by the men, he told a ghost story that set the women to looking back over their shoulders into the dark corners beyond the zone of candle-light. All of us, I remember, except Sperry and Mrs. Dane, were skeptical as to the supernatural, and Herbert Robinson believed that while there were so-called sensitives who actually went into trance, the controls which took possession of them were buried personalities of their own, released during trance from the sub-conscious mind.

"If not," he said truculently, "if they are really spirits, why can't they tell us what is going on, not in some vague place where they are always happy, but here and now, in the next house? I don't ask for prophecy, but for some evidence of their knowledge. Are the Germans getting ready to fight England? Is Horace here the gay dog some of us suspect?"

As I am the Horace in question, I must explain that Herbert was merely being facetious. My life is a most orderly and decorous one. But my wife, unfortunately, lacks a sense of humor, and I felt that the remark might have been more fortunate.

"Physical phenomena!" scoffed the cynic. "I've seen it all— objects moving without visible hands, unexplained currents of cold air, voice through a trumpet—I know the whole rotten mess, and I've got a book which tells how to do all the tricks. I'll bring it along some night."

Mrs. Dane smiled, and the discussion was dropped for a time. It was during the coffee and cigars that Mrs. Dane made her announcement. As Alice Robinson takes an after-dinner cigarette, a custom my wife greatly deplores, the ladies had remained with us at the table.

"As a matter of fact, Herbert," she said, "we intend to put your skepticism to the test tonight. Doctor Sperry has found a medium for us, a non-professional and a patient of his, and she has kindly consented to give us a sitting."

Herbert wheeled and looked at Sperry.

"Hold up your right hand and state by your honor as a member in good standing that you have not primed her, Sperry."

Sperry held up his hand.

"Absolutely not," he said, gravely. "She is coming in my car. She doesn't know to what house or whose. She knows none of you. She is a stranger to the city, and she will not even recognize the neighborhood."

II

The butler wheeled out Mrs. Dane's chair, as her companion did not dine with her on club nights, and led us to the drawing-room doors. There Sperry threw them, open, and we saw that the room had been completely metamorphosed.

Mrs. Dane's drawing-room is generally rather painful. Kindly soul that she is, she has considered it necessary to preserve and exhibit there the many gifts of a long lifetime. Photographs long outgrown, onyx tables, a clutter of odd chairs and groups of discordant bric-a-brac usually make the progress of her chair through it a precarious and perilous matter. We paused in the doorway, startled.

The room had been dismantled. It opened before us, walls and chimney-piece bare, rugs gone from the floor, even curtains taken from the windows. To emphasize the change, in the center stood a common pine table, surrounded by seven plain chairs. All the lights were out save one, a corner bracket, which was screened with a red-paper shade.

She watched our faces with keen satisfaction. "Such a time I had doing it!" she said. "The servants, of course, think I have gone mad. All except Clara. I told her. She's a sensible girl."

Herbert chuckled.

"Very neat," he said, "although a chair or two for the spooks would have been no more than hospitable. All right. Now bring on your ghosts."

My wife, however, looked slightly displeased. "As a church-woman," she said, "I really feel that it is positively impious to bring back the souls of the departed, before they are called from on High."

"Oh, rats," Herbert broke in rudely. "They'll not come. Don't worry. And if you hear raps, don't worry. It will probably be the medium cracking the joint of her big toe."

There was still a half hour until the medium's arrival. At Mrs. Dane's direction we employed it in searching the room. It was the ordinary rectangular drawing-room, occupying a corner of the house. Two windows at the end faced on the street, with a patch of railed-in lawn beneath them. A fire-place with a dying fire and flanked by two other windows, occupied the long side opposite the door into the hall. These windows, opening on a garden, were closed by outside shutters, now bolted. The third side was a blank wall, beyond which lay the library. On the fourth side were the double doors into the hall.

As, although the results we obtained were far beyond any expectations, the purely physical phenomena were relatively insignificant, it is not necessary to go further into the detail of the room. Robinson has done that, anyhow, for the Society of Psychical Research, a proceeding to which I was opposed, as will be understood by the close of the narrative.

Further to satisfy Mrs. Dane, we examined the walls and floor-boards carefully, and Herbert, armed with a candle, went down to the cellar and investigated from below, returning to announce in a loud voice which made us all jump that it seemed all clear enough down there. After that we sat and waited, and I daresay the bareness and darkness of the room put us into excellent receptive condition. I know that I myself, probably owing to an astigmatism, once or twice felt that I saw wavering shadows in corners, and I felt again some of the strangeness I had felt during the day. We spoke in whispers, and Alice Robinson recited the history of a haunted house where she had visited in England. But Herbert was still cynical. He said, I remember:

"Here we are, six intelligent persons of above the average grade, and in a few minutes our hair will be rising and our pulses hammering while a Choctaw Indian control, in atrocious English, will tell us she is happy and we are happy and so everybody's happy. Hanky panky!"

"You may be as skeptical as you please, if you will only be fair, Herbert," Mrs. Dane said.

"And by that you mean—"

"During the sitting keep an open mind and a closed mouth," she replied, cheerfully.

As I said at the beginning, this is not a ghost story. Parts of it we now understand, other parts we do not. For the physical phenomena we have no adequate explanation. They occurred. We saw and heard them. For the other part of the seance we have come to a conclusion satisfactory to ourselves, a conclusion not reached, however, until some of us had gone through some dangerous experiences, and had been brought into contact with things hitherto outside the orderly progression of our lives.

But at no time, although incredible things happened, did any one of us glimpse that strange world of the spirit that seemed so often almost within our range of vision.

Miss Jeremy, the medium, was due at 8:30 and at 8:20 my wife assisted Mrs. Dane into one of the straight chairs at the table, and Sperry, sent out by her, returned with a darkish bundle in his arms, and carrying a light bamboo rod.

"Don't ask me what they are for," he said to Herbert's grin of amusement. "Every workman has his tools."

Herbert examined the rod, but it was what it appeared to be, and nothing else.

Some one had started the phonograph in the library, and it was playing gloomily, "Shall we meet beyond the river?" At Sperry's request we stopped talking and composed ourselves, and Herbert, I remember, took a tablet of some sort, to our intense annoyance, and crunched it in his teeth. Then Miss Jeremy came in.

She was not at all what we had expected. Twenty-six, I should say, and in a black dinner dress. She seemed like a perfectly normal young woman, even attractive in a fragile, delicate way. Not much personality, perhaps; the very word "medium" precludes that. A "sensitive," I think she called herself. We were presented to her, and but for the stripped and bare room, it might have been any evening after any dinner, with bridge waiting.

When she shook hands with me she looked at me keenly. "What a strange day it has been!" she said. "I have been very nervous. I only hope I can do what you want this evening."

"I am not at all sure what we do want, Miss Jeremy," I replied.

She smiled a quick smile that was not without humor. Somehow I had never thought of a medium with a sense of humor. I liked her at once. We all liked her, and Sperry, Sperry the bachelor, the iconoclast, the antifeminist, was staring at her with curiously intent eyes.

Following her entrance Herbert had closed and bolted the drawing-room doors, and as an added precaution he now drew Mrs. Dane's empty wheeled chair across them.

"Anything that comes in," he boasted, "will come through the keyhole or down the chimney."

And then, eying the fireplace, he deliberately took a picture from the wall and set it on the fender.

Miss Jeremy gave the room only the most casual of glances.

"Where shall I sit?" she asked.

Mrs. Dane indicated her place, and she asked for a small stand to be brought in and placed about two feet behind her chair, and two chairs to flank it, and then to take the black cloth from the table and hang it over the bamboo rod, which was laid across the backs of the chairs. Thus arranged, the curtain formed a low screen behind her, with the stand beyond it. On this stand we placed, at her order, various articles from our pockets—I a fountain pen, Sperry a knife; and my wife contributed a gold bracelet.

We all felt, I fancy, rather absurd. Herbert's smile in the dim light became a grin. "The same old thing!" he whispered to me. "Watch her closely. They do it with a folding rod."

We arranged between us that we were to sit one on each side of her, and Sperry warned me not to let go of her hand for a moment. "They have a way of switching hands," he explained in a whisper. "If she wants to scratch her nose I'll scratch it."

We were, we discovered, not to touch the table, but to sit around it at a distance of a few inches, holding hands and thus forming the circle. And for twenty minutes we sat thus, and nothing happened. She was fully conscious and even spoke once or twice, and at last she moved impatiently and told us to put our hands on the table.

I had put my opened watch on the table before me, a night watch with a luminous dial. At five minutes after nine I felt the top of the table waver under my fingers, a curious, fluid-like motion.

"The table is going to move," I said.

Herbert laughed, a dry little chuckle. "Sure it is," he said. "When we all get to acting together, it will probably do considerable moving. I feel what you feel. It's flowing under my fingers."

"Blood," said Sperry. "You fellows feel the blood moving through the ends of your fingers. That's all. Don't be impatient."

However, curiously enough, the table did not move. Instead, my watch, before my eyes, slid to the edge of the table and dropped to the floor, and almost instantly an object, which we recognized later as Sperry's knife, was flung over the curtain and struck the wall behind Mrs. Dane violently.

One of the women screamed, ending in a hysterical giggle. Then we heard rhythmic beating on the top of the stand behind the medium. Startling as it was at the beginning, increasing as it did from a slow beat to an incredibly rapid drumming, when the initial shock was over Herbert commenced to gibe.

"Your fountain pen, Horace," he said to me. "Making out a statement for services rendered, by its eagerness."

The answer to that was the pen itself, aimed at him with apparent accuracy, and followed by an outcry from him.

"Here, stop it!" he said. "I've got ink all over me!"

We laughed consumedly. The sitting had taken on all the attributes of practical joking. The table no longer quivered under my hands.

"Please be sure you are holding my hands tight. Hold them very tight," said Miss Jeremy. Her voice sounded faint and far away. Her head was dropped forward on her chest, and she suddenly sagged in her chair. Sperry broke the circle and coming to her, took her pulse. It was, he reported, very rapid.

"You can move and talk now if you like," he said. "She's in trance, and there will be no more physical demonstrations."

Mrs. Dane was the first to speak. I was looking for my fountain pen, and Herbert was again examining the stand.

"I believe it now," Mrs. Dane said. "I saw your watch go, Horace, but tomorrow I won't believe it at all."

"How about your companion?" I asked. "Can she take shorthand? We ought to have a record."

"Probably not in the dark."

"We can have some light now," Sperry said.

There was a sort of restrained movement in the room now. Herbert turned on a bracket light, and I moved away the roller chair.

"Go and get Clara, Horace," Mrs. Dane said to me, "and have her bring a note-book and pencil." Nothing, I believe, happened during my absence. Miss Jeremy was sunk in her chair and breathing heavily when I came back with Clara, and Sperry was still watching her pulse. Suddenly my wife said:

"Why, look! She's wearing my bracelet!"

This proved to be the case, and was, I regret to say, the cause of a most unjust suspicion on my wife's part. Even today, with all the knowledge she possesses, I am certain that Mrs. Johnson believes that some mysterious power took my watch and dragged it off the table, and threw the pen, but that I myself under cover of darkness placed her bracelet on Miss Jeremy's arm. I can only reiterate here what I have told her many times, that I never touched the bracelet after it was placed on the stand.

"Take down everything that happens, Clara, and all we say," Mrs. Dane said in a low tone. "Even if it sounds like nonsense, put it down."

It is because Clara took her orders literally that I am making this more readable version of her script. There was a certain amount of non-pertinent matter which would only cloud the statement if rendered word for word, and also certain scattered, unrelated words with which many of the statements terminated. For instance, at the end of the sentence, "Just above the ear," came a number of rhymes to the final word, "dear, near, fear, rear, cheer, three cheers." These I have cut, for the sake of clearness.

For some five minutes, perhaps, Miss Jeremy breathed stertorously, and it was during that interval that we introduced Clara and took up our positions. Sperry sat near the medium now, having changed places with Herbert, and the rest of us were as we had been, save that we no longer touched hands. Suddenly Miss Jeremy began to breathe more quietly, and to move about in her chair. Then she sat upright.

"Good evening, friends," she said. "I am glad to see you all again."

I caught Herbert's eye, and he grinned.

"Good evening, little Bright Eyes," he said. "How's everything in the happy hunting ground tonight?"

"Dark and cold," she said. "Dark and cold. And the knee hurts. It's very bad. If the key is on the nail—Arnica will take the pain out."

She lapsed into silence. In transcribing Clara's record I shall make no reference to these pauses, which were frequent, and occasionally filled in with extraneous matter. For instance, once there was what amounted to five minutes of Mother Goose jingles. Our method was simply one of question, by one of ourselves, and of answer by Miss Jeremy. These replies were usually in a querulous tone, and were often apparently unwilling. Also occasionally there was a bit of vernacular, as in the next reply. Herbert, who was still flippantly amused, said:

"Don't bother about your knee. Give us some local stuff. Gossip. If you can."

"Sure I can, and it will make your hair curl." Then suddenly there was a sort of dramatic pause and then an outburst.

"He's dead."

"Who is dead?" Sperry asked, with his voice drawn a trifle thin.

"A bullet just above the ear. That's a bad place. Thank goodness there's not much blood. Cold water will take it out of the carpet. Not hot. Not hot. Do you want to set the stain?"

"Look here," Sperry said, looking around the table. "I don't like this. It's darned grisly."

"Oh, fudge!" Herbert put in irreverently. "Let her rave, or it, or whatever it is. Do you mean that a man is dead?"—to the medium.

"Yes. She has the revolver. She needn't cry so. He was cruel to her. He was a beast. Sullen."

"Can you see the woman?" I asked.

"If it's sent out to be cleaned it will cause trouble. Hang it in the closet."

Herbert muttered something about the movies having nothing on us, and was angrily hushed. There was something quite outside of Miss Jeremy's words that had impressed itself on all of us with a sense of unexpected but very real tragedy. As I look back I believe it was a sort of desperation in her voice. But then came one of those interruptions which were to annoy us considerably during the series of sittings; she began to recite Childe Harold.

When that was over,

"Now then," Sperry said in a businesslike voice, "you see a dead man, and a young woman with him. Can you describe the room?"

"A small room, his dressing-room. He was shaving. There is still lather on his face."

"And the woman killed him?"

"I don't know. Oh, I don't know. No, she didn't. He did it!"

"He did it himself?"

There was no answer to that, but a sort of sulky silence.

"Are you getting this, Clara?" Mrs. Dane asked sharply. "Don't miss a word. Who knows what this may develop into?"

I looked at the secretary, and it was clear that she was terrified. I got up and took my chair to her. Coming back, I picked up my forgotten watch from the floor. It was still going, and the hands marked nine-thirty.

"Now," Sperry said in a soothing tone, "you said there was a shot fired and a man was killed. Where was this? What house?"

"Two shots. One is in the ceiling of the dressing-room."

"And the other killed him?"

But here, instead of a reply we got the words, "library paste."

Quite without warning the medium groaned, and Sperry believed the trance was over.

"She's coming out," he said. "A glass of wine, somebody." But she did not come out. Instead, she twisted in the chair.

"He's so heavy to lift," she muttered. Then: "Get the lather off his face. The lather. The lather."

She subsided into the chair and began to breathe with difficulty. "I want to go out. I want air. If I could only go to sleep and forget it. The drawing-room furniture is scattered over the house."

This last sentence she repeated over and over. It got on our nerves, ragged already.

"Can you tell us about the house?"

There was a distinct pause. Then: "Certainly. A brick house. The servants' entrance is locked, but the key is on a nail, among the vines. All the furniture is scattered through the house."

"She must mean the furniture of this room," Mrs. Dane whispered.

The remainder of the sitting was chaotic. The secretary's notes consist of unrelated words and often childish verses. On going over the notes the next day, when the stenographic record had been copied on a typewriter, Sperry and I found that one word recurred frequently. The word was "curtain." Of the extraordinary event that followed the breaking up of the seance, I have the keenest recollection. Miss Jeremy came out of her trance weak and looking extremely ill, and Sperry's motor took her home. She knew nothing of what had happened, and hoped we had been satisfied. By agreement, we did not tell her what had transpired, and she was not curious.

Herbert saw her to the car, and came back, looking grave. We were standing together in the center of the dismantled room, with the lights going full now.

"Well," he said, "it is one of two things. Either we've been gloriously faked, or we've been let in on a very tidy little crime."

It was Mrs. Dane's custom to serve a Southern eggnog as a sort of stir-up-cup—nightcap, she calls it—on her evenings, and we found it waiting for us in the library. In the warmth of its open fire, and the cheer of its lamps, even in the dignity and impassiveness of the butler, there was something sane and wholesome. The women of the party reacted quickly, but I looked over to see Sperry at a corner desk, intently working over a small object in the palm of his hand.

He started when he heard me, then laughed and held out his hand.

"Library paste!" he said. "It rolls into a soft, malleable ball. It could quite easily be used to fill a small hole in plaster. The paper would paste down over it, too."

"Then you think?"

"I'm not thinking at all. The thing she described may have taken place in Timbuctoo. May have happened ten years ago. May be the plot of some book she has read."

"On the other hand," I replied, "it is just possible that it was here, in this neighborhood, while we were sitting in that room."

"Have you any idea of the time?"

"I know exactly. It was half-past nine."

III

At midnight, shortly after we reached home, Sperry called me on the phone. "Be careful, Horace," he said. "Don't let Mrs. Horace think anything has happened. I want to see you at once. Suppose you say I have a patient in a bad way, and a will to be drawn."

I listened to sounds from upstairs. I heard my wife go into her room and close the door.

"Tell me something about it," I urged.

"Just this. Arthur Wells killed himself tonight, shot himself in the head. I want you to go there with me."

"Arthur Wells!"

"Yes. I say, Horace, did you happen to notice the time the seance began tonight?"

"It was five minutes after nine when my watch fell."

"Then it would have been about half past when the trance began?"

"Yes."

There was a silence at Sperry's end of the wire. Then:

"He was shot about 9:30," he said, and rang off.

I am not ashamed to confess that my hands shook as I hung up the receiver. A brick house, she had said; the Wells house was brick. And so were all the other houses on the street. Vines in the back? Well, even my own house had vines. It was absurd; it was pure coincidence; it was—well, I felt it was queer.

Nevertheless, as I stood there, I wondered for the first time in a highly material existence, whether there might not be, after all, a spirit-world surrounding us, cognizant of all that we did, touching but intangible, sentient but tuned above our common senses?

I stood by the prosaic telephone instrument and looked into the darkened recesses of the passage. It seemed to my disordered nerves that back of the coats and wraps that hung on the rack, beyond the heavy curtains, in every corner, there lurked vague and shadowy forms, invisible when I stared, but advancing a trifle from their obscurity when, by turning my head and looking ahead, they impinged on the extreme right or left of my field of vision.

I was shocked by the news, but not greatly grieved. The Wellses had been among us but not of us, as I have said. They had come, like gay young comets, into our orderly constellation, trailing behind them their cars and servants, their children and governesses and rather riotous friends, and had flashed on us in a sort of bright impermanence.

Of the two, I myself had preferred Arthur. His faults were on the surface. He drank hard, gambled, and could not always pay his gambling debts. But underneath it all there had always been something boyishly honest about him. He had played, it is true, through most of the thirty years that now marked his whole life, but he could have been made a man by the right woman. And he had married the wrong one.

Of Elinor Wells I have only my wife's verdict, and I have found that, as is the way with many good women, her judgments of her own sex are rather merciless. A tall, handsome girl, very dark, my wife has characterized her as cold, calculating and ambitious. She has said frequently, too, that Elinor Wells was a disappointed woman, that her marriage, while giving her social identity, had disappointed her in a monetary way. Whether that is true or not, there was no doubt, by the time they had lived in our neighborhood for a year, that a complication had arisen in the shape of another man.

My wife, on my return from my office in the evening, had been quite likely to greet me with:

"Horace, he has been there all afternoon. I really think something should be done about it."

"Who has been where?" I would ask, I am afraid not too patiently.

"You know perfectly well. And I think you ought to tell him."

In spite of her vague pronouns, I understood, and in a more masculine way I shared her sense of outrage. Our street has never had a scandal on it, except the one when the Berringtons' music teacher ran away with their coachman, in the days of carriages. And I am glad to say that that is almost forgotten.

Nevertheless, we had realized for some time that the dreaded triangle was threatening the repute of our quiet neighborhood, and as I stood by the telephone that night I saw that it had come. More than that, it seemed very probable that into this very triangle our peaceful Neighborhood Club had been suddenly thrust.

My wife accepted my excuse coldly. She dislikes intensely the occasional outside calls of my profession. She merely observed, however, that she would leave all the lights on until my return. "I should think you could arrange things better, Horace," she added. "It's perfectly idiotic the way people die at night. And tonight, of all nights!"

I shall have to confess that through all of the thirty years of our married life my wife has clung to the belief that I am a bit of a dog. Thirty years of exemplary living have not affected this conviction, nor had Herbert's foolish remark earlier in the evening helped matters. But she watched me put on my overcoat without further comment. When I kissed her good-night, however, she turned her cheek.

The street, with its open spaces, was a relief after the dark hall. I started for Sperry's house, my head bent against the wind, my mind on the news I had just heard. Was it, I wondered, just possible that we had for some reason been allowed behind the veil which covered poor Wells' last moments? And, to admit that for a moment, where would what we had heard lead us? Sperry had said he had killed himself. But—suppose he had not?

I realize now, looking back, that my recollection of the other man in the triangle is largely colored by the fact that he fell in the great war. At that time I hardly knew him, except as a wealthy and self-made man in his late thirties; I saw him now and then, in the club playing billiards or going in and out of the Wells house, a large, fastidiously dressed man, strong featured and broad shouldered, with rather too much manner. I remember particularly how I hated the light spats he affected, and the glaring yellow gloves.

A man who would go straight for the thing he wanted, woman or power or money. And get it.

Sperry was waiting on his door-step, and we went on to the Wells house. What with the magnitude of the thing that had happened, and our mutual feeling that we were somehow involved in it, we were rather silent. Sperry asked one question, however, "Are you certain about the time when Miss Jeremy saw what looks like this thing?"

"Certainly. My watch fell at five minutes after nine. When it was all over, and I picked it up, it was still going, and it was 9:30."

He was silent for a moment. Then:

"The Wellses' nursery governess telephoned for me at 9:35. We keep a record of the time of all calls."

Sperry is a heart specialist, I think I have said, with offices in his house.

And, a block or so farther on: "I suppose it was bound to come. To tell the truth, I didn't think the boy had the courage."

"Then you think he did it?"

"They say so," he said grimly. And added,—irritably: "Good heavens, Horace, we must keep that other fool thing out of our minds."

"Yes," I agreed. "We must."

Although the Wells house was brilliantly lighted when we reached it, we had difficulty in gaining admission. Whoever were in the house were up-stairs, and the bell evidently rang in the deserted kitchen or a neighboring pantry.

"We might try the servants' entrance," Sperry said. Then he laughed mirthlessly.

"We might see," he said, "if there's a key on the nail among the vines."

I confess to a nervous tightening of my muscles as we made our way around the house. If the key was there, we were on the track of a revelation that might revolutionize much that we had held fundamental in science and in our knowledge of life itself. If, sitting in Mrs. Dane's quiet room, a woman could tell us what was happening in a house a mile or so away, it opened up a new earth. Almost a new heaven.

I stopped and touched Sperry's arm. "This Miss Jeremy—did she know Arthur Wells or Elinor? If she knew the house, and the situation between them, isn't it barely possible that she anticipated this thing?"

"We knew them," he said gruffly, "and whatever we anticipated, it wasn't this."

Sperry had a pocket flash, and when we found the door locked we proceeded with our search for the key. The porch had been covered with heavy vines, now dead of the November frosts, and showing, here and there, dead and dried leaves that crackled as we touched them. In the darkness something leaped against, me, and I almost cried out. It was, however, only a collie dog, eager for the warmth of his place by the kitchen fire.

"Here's the key," Sperry said, and held it out. The flash wavered in his hand, and his voice was strained.

"So far, so good," I replied, and was conscious that my own voice rang strange in my ears.

We admitted ourselves, and the dog, bounding past us, gave a sharp yelp of gratitude and ran into the kitchen.

"Look here, Sperry," I said, as we stood inside the door, "they don't want me here. They've sent for you, but I'm the most casual sort of an acquaintance. I haven't any business here."

That struck him, too. We had both been so obsessed with the scene at Mrs. Dane's that we had not thought of anything else.

"Suppose you sit down in the library," he said. "The chances are against her coming down, and the servants don't matter."

As a matter of fact, we learned later that all the servants were out except the nursery governess. There were two small children. There was a servants' ball somewhere, and, with the exception of the butler, it was after two before they commenced to straggle in. Except two plain-clothes men from the central office, a physician who was with Elinor in her room, and the governess, there was no one else in the house but the children, asleep in the nursery.

As I sat alone in the library, the house was perfectly silent. But in some strange fashion it had apparently taken on the attributes of the deed that had preceded the silence. It was sinister, mysterious, dark. Its immediate effect on my imagination was apprehension—almost terror. Murder or suicide, here among the shadows a soul, an indestructible thing, had been recently violently wrenched from its body. The body lay in the room overhead. But what of the spirit? I shivered as I thought that it might even then be watching me with formless eyes from some dark corner.

Overwrought as I was, I was forced to bring my common sense to bear on the situation. Here was a tragedy, a real and terrible one. Suppose we had, in some queer fashion, touched its outer edges that night? Then how was it that there had come, mixed up with so much that might be pertinent, such extraneous and grotesque things as Childe Harold, a hurt knee, and Mother Goose?

I remember moving impatiently, and trying to argue myself into my ordinary logical state of mind, but I know now that even then I was wondering whether Sperry had found a hole in the ceiling upstairs.

I wandered, I recall, into the realm of the clairvoyant and the clairaudient. Under certain conditions, such as trance, I knew that some individuals claimed a power of vision that was supernormal, and I had at one time lunched at my club with a well-dressed gentleman in a pince nez who said the room was full of people I could not see, but who were perfectly distinct to him. He claimed, and I certainly could not refute him, that he saw further into the violet of the spectrum than the rest of us, and seemed to consider it nothing unusual when an elderly woman, whose description sounded much like my great-grand-mother, came and stood behind my chair.

I recall that he said she was stroking my hair, and that following that I had a distinctly creepy sensation along my scalp.

Then there were those who claimed that in trance the spirit of the medium, giving place to a control, was free to roam whither it would, and, although I am not sure of this, that it wandered in the fourth dimension. While I am very vague about the fourth dimension, I did know that in it doors and walls were not obstacles. But as they would not be obstacles to a spirit, even in the world as we know it, that got me nowhere.

Suppose Sperry came down and said Arthur Wells had been shot above the ear, and that there was a second bullet hole in the ceiling? Added to the key on the nail, a careless custom and surely not common, we would have conclusive proof that our medium had been correct. There was another point, too. Miss Jeremy had said, "Get the lather off his face."

That brought me up with a turn. Would a man stop shaving to kill himself? If he did, why a revolver? Why not the razor in his hand?

I knew from my law experience that suicide is either a desperate impulse or a cold-blooded and calculated finality. A man who kills himself while dressing comes under the former classification, and will usually seize the first method at hand. But there was something else, too. Shaving is an automatic process. It completes itself. My wife has an irritated conviction that if the house caught fire while I was in the midst of the process, I would complete it and rinse the soap from my face before I caught up the fire-extinguisher.

Had he killed himself, or had Elinor killed him? Was she the sort to sacrifice herself to a violent impulse? Would she choose the hard way, when there was the easy one of the divorce court? I thought not. And the same was true of Ellingham. Here were two people, both of them careful of appearance, if not of fact. There was another possibility, too. That he had learned something while he was dressing, had attacked or threatened her with a razor, and she had killed him in self-defence.

I had reached that point when Sperry came down the staircase, ushering out the detectives and the medical man. He came to the library door and stood looking at me, with his face rather paler than usual.

"I'll take you up now," he said. "She's in her room, in bed, and she has had an opiate."

"Was he shot above the ear?"

"Yes."

I did not look at him, nor he at me. We climbed the stairs and entered the room, where, according to Elinor's story, Arthur Wells had killed himself. It was a dressing-room, as Miss Jeremy had described. A wardrobe, a table with books and magazines in disorder, two chairs, and a couch, constituted the furnishings. Beyond was a bathroom. On a chair by a window the dead mans's evening clothes were neatly laid out, his shoes beneath. His top hat and folded gloves were on the table.

Arthur Wells lay on the couch. A sheet had been drawn over the body, and I did not disturb it. It gave the impression of unusual length that is always found, I think, in the dead, and a breath of air from an open window, by stirring the sheet, gave a false appearance of life beneath.

The house was absolutely still.

When I glanced at Sperry he was staring at the ceiling, and I followed his eyes, but there was no mark on it. Sperry made a little gesture.

"It's queer," he muttered. "It's—"

"The detective and I put him there. He was here." He showed a place on the floor midway of the room.

"Where was his head lying?" I asked, cautiously.

"Here."

I stooped and examined the carpet. It was a dark Oriental, with much red in it. I touched the place, and then ran my folded handkerchief over it. It came up stained with blood.

"There would be no object in using cold water there, so as not to set the stain," Sperry said thoughtfully. "Whether he fell there or not, that is where she allowed him to be found."

"You don't think he fell there?"

"She dragged him, didn't she?" he demanded. Then the strangeness of what he was saying struck him, and he smiled foolishly. "What I mean is, the medium said she did. I don't suppose any jury would pass us tonight as entirely sane, Horace," he said.

He walked across to the bathroom and surveyed it from the doorway. I followed him. It was as orderly as the other room. On a glass shelf over the wash-stand were his razors, a safety and, beside it, in a black case, an assortment of the long-bladed variety, one for each day of the week, and so marked.

Sperry stood thoughtfully in the doorway.

"The servants are out," he said. "According to Elinor's statement he was dressing when he did it. And yet some one has had a wild impulse for tidiness here, since it happened. Not a towel out of place!"

It was in the bathroom that he told me Elinor's story. According to her, it was a simple case of suicide. And she was honest about it, in her own way. She was shocked, but she was not pretending any wild grief. She hadn't wanted him to die, but she had not felt that they could go on much longer together. There had been no quarrel other than their usual bickering. They had been going to a dance that night. The servants had all gone out immediately after dinner to a servants' ball and the governess had gone for a walk. She was to return at nine-thirty to fasten Elinor's gown and to be with the children.

Arthur, she said, had been depressed for several days, and at dinner had hardly spoken at all. He had not, however, objected to the dance. He had, indeed, seemed strangely determined to go, although she had pleaded a headache. At nine o'clock he went upstairs, apparently to dress.

She was in her room, with the door shut, when she heard a shot. She ran in and found him lying on the floor of his dressing-room with his revolver behind him. The governess was still out. The shot had roused the children, and they had come down from the nursery above. She was frantic, but she had to soothe them. The governess, however, came in almost immediately, and she had sent her to the telephone to summon help, calling Sperry first of all, and then the police.

"Have you seen the revolver?" I asked.

"Yes. It's all right, apparently. Only one shot had been fired."

"How soon did they get a doctor?"

"It must have been some time. They gave up telephoning, and the governess went out, finally, and found one."

"Then, while she was out—?"

"Possibly," Sperry said. "If we start with the hypothesis that she was lying."

"If she cleaned up here for any reason," I began, and commenced a desultory examination of the room. Just why I looked behind the bathtub forces me to an explanation I am somewhat loath to make, but which will explain a rather unusual proceeding. For some time my wife has felt that I smoked too heavily, and out of her solicitude for me has limited me to one cigar after dinner. But as I have been a heavy smoker for years I have found this a great hardship, and have therefore kept a reserve store, by arrangement with the housemaid, behind my tub. In self-defence I must also state that I seldom have recourse to such stealthy measures.

Believing then that something might possibly be hidden there, I made an investigation, and could see some small objects lying there. Sperry brought me a stick from the dressing-room, and with its aid succeeded in bringing out the two articles which were instrumental in starting us on our brief but adventurous careers as private investigators. One was a leather razor strop, old and stiff from disuse, and the other a wet bath sponge, now stained with blood to a yellowish brown.

"She is lying, Sperry," I said. "He fell somewhere else, and she dragged him to where he was found."

"But—why?"

"I don't know," I said impatiently. "From some place where a man would be unlikely to kill himself, I daresay. No one ever killed himself, for instance, in an open hallway. Or stopped shaving to do it."

"We have only Miss Jeremy's word for that," he said, sullenly. "Confound it, Horace, don't let's bring in that stuff if we can help it."

We stared at each other, with the strop and the sponge between us. Suddenly he turned on his heel and went back into the room, and a moment later he called me, quietly.

"You're right," he said. "The poor devil was shaving. He had it half done. Come and look."

But I did not go. There was a carafe of water in the bathroom, and I took a drink from it. My hands were shaking. When I turned around I found Sperry in the hall, examining the carpet with his flash light, and now and then stooping to run his hand over the floor.

"Nothing here," he said in a low tone, when I had joined him. "At least I haven't found anything."

IV

How much of Sperry's proceeding with the carpet the governess had seen I do not know. I glanced up and she was there, on the staircase to the third floor, watching us. I did not know, then, whether she recognized me or not, for the Wellses' servants were as oblivious of the families on the street as their employers. But she knew Sperry, and was ready enough to talk to him.

"How is she now?" she asked.

"She is sleeping, Mademoiselle."

"The children also."

She came down the stairs, a lean young Frenchwoman in a dark dressing gown, and Sperry suggested that she too should have an opiate. She seized at the idea, but Sperry did not go down at once for his professional bag.

"You were not here when it occurred, Mademoiselle?" he inquired.

"No, doctor. I had been out for a walk." She clasped her hands. "When I came back——"

"Was he still on the floor of the dressing-room when you came in?"

"But yes. Of course. She was alone. She could not lift him."

"I see," Sperry said thoughtfully. "No, I daresay she couldn't. Was the revolver on the floor also?"

"Yes, doctor. I myself picked it up."

To Sperry she showed, I observed, a slight deference, but when she glanced at me, as she did after each reply, I thought her expression slightly altered. At the time this puzzled me, but it was explained when Sperry started down the stairs.

"Monsieur is of the police?" she asked, with a Frenchwoman's timid respect for the constabulary.

I hesitated before I answered. I am a truthful man, and I hate unnecessary lying. But I ask consideration of the circumstances.

Neither then nor at any time later was the solving of the Wells mystery the prime motive behind the course I laid out and consistently followed. I felt that we might be on the verge of some great psychic discovery, one which would revolutionize human thought and to a certain extent human action. And toward that end I was prepared to go to almost any length.

"I am making a few investigations," I told her. "You say Mrs. Wells was alone in the house, except for her husband?"

"The children."

"Mr. Wells was shaving, I believe, when the—er—impulse overtook him?"

There was no doubt as to her surprise. "Shaving? I think not."

"What sort of razor did he ordinarily use?"

"A safety razor always. At least I have never seen any others around."

"There is a case of old-fashioned razors in the bathroom."

She glanced toward the room and shrugged her shoulders. "Possibly he used others. I have not seen any."

"It was you, I suppose, who cleaned up afterwards."

"Cleaned up?"

"You who washed up the stains."

"Stains? Oh, no, monsieur. Nothing of the sort has yet been done."

I felt that she was telling the truth, so far as she knew it, and I then asked about the revolver.

"Do you know where Mr. Wells kept his revolver?"

"When I first came it was in the drawer of that table. I suggested that it be placed beyond the children's reach. I do not know where it was put."

"Do you recall how you left the front door when you went out? I mean, was it locked?"

"No. The servants were out, and I knew there would be no one to admit me. I left it unfastened."

But it was evident that she had broken a rule of the house by doing so, for she added: "I am afraid to use the servants' entrance. It is dark there."

"The key is always hung on the nail when they are out?"

"Yes. If any one of them is out it is left there. There is only one key. The family is out a great deal, and it saves bringing some one down from the servants' rooms at the top of the house."

But I think my knowledge of the key bothered her, for some reason. And as I read over my questions, certainly they indicated a suspicion that the situation was less simple than it appeared. She shot a quick glance at me.

"Did you examine the revolver when you picked it up?"

"I, monsieur? Non!" Then her fears, whatever they were, got the best of her. "I know nothing but what I tell you. I was out. I can prove that that is so. I went to a pharmacy; the clerk will remember. I will go with you, monsieur, and he will tell you that I used the telephone there."

I daresay my business of cross-examination, of watching evidence helped me to my next question.

"You went out to telephone when there is a telephone in the house?"

But here again, as once or twice before, a veil dropped between us. She avoided my eyes. "There are things one does not want the family to hear," she muttered. Then, having determined on a course of action, she followed it. "I am looking for another position. I do not like it here. The children are spoiled. I only came for a month's trial."

"And the pharmacy?"

"Elliott's, at the corner of State Avenue and McKee Street."

I told her that it would not be necessary for her to go to the pharmacy, and she muttered something about the children and went up the stairs. When Sperry came back with the opiate she was nowhere in sight, and he was considerably annoyed.

"She knows something," I told him. "She is frightened."

Sperry eyed me with a half frown.

"Now see here, Horace," he said, "suppose we had come in here, without the thought of that seance behind us? We'd have accepted the thing as it appears to be, wouldn't we? There may be a dozen explanations for that sponge, and for the razor strop. What in heaven's name has a razor strop to do with it anyhow? One bullet was fired, and the revolver has one empty chamber. It may not be the custom to stop shaving in order to commit suicide, but that's no argument that it can't be done, and as to the key—how do I know that my own back door key isn't hung outside on a nail sometimes?"

"We might look again for that hole in the ceiling."

"I won't do it. Miss Jeremy has read of something of that sort, or heard of it, and stored it in her subconscious mind."

But he glanced up at the ceiling nevertheless, and a moment later had drawn up a chair and stepped onto it, and I did the same thing. We presented, I imagine, rather a strange picture, and I know that the presence of the rigid figure on the couch gave me a sort of ghoulish feeling.

The house was an old one, and in the center of the high ceiling a plaster ornament surrounded the chandelier. Our search gradually centered on this ornament, but the chairs were low and our long-distance examination revealed nothing. It was at that time, too, that we heard some one in the lower hall, and we had only a moment to put our chairs in place before the butler came in. He showed no surprise, but stood looking at the body on the couch, his thin face working.

"I met the detectives outside, doctor," he said. "It's a terrible thing, sir, a terrible thing."

"I'd keep the other servants out of this room, Hawkins."

"Yes, sir." He went over to the sheet, lifted the edge slowly, and then replaced it, and tip-toed to the door. "The others are not back yet. I'll admit them, and get them up quietly. How is Mrs. Wells?"

"Sleeping," Sperry said briefly, and Hawkins went out.

I realize now that Sperry was—I am sure he will forgive this—in a state of nerves that night. For example, he returned only an impatient silence to my doubt as to whether Hawkins had really only just returned and he quite missed something downstairs which I later proved to have an important bearing on the case. This was when we were going out, and after Hawkins had opened the front door for us. It had been freezing hard, and Sperry, who has a bad ankle, looked about for a walking stick. He found one, and I saw Hawkins take a swift step forward, and then stop, with no expression whatever in his face.

"This will answer, Hawkins."

"Yes, sir," said Hawkins impassively.

And if I realize that Sperry was nervous that night, I also realize that he was fighting a battle quite his own, and with its personal problems.

"She's got to quit this sort of thing," he said savagely and apropos of nothing, as we walked along. "It's hard on her, and besides—"

"Yes?"

"She couldn't have learned about it," he said, following his own trail of thought. "My car brought her from her home to the house-door. She was brought in to us at once. But don't you see that if there are other developments, to prove her statements she—well, she's as innocent as a child, but take Herbert, for instance. Do you suppose he'll believe she had no outside information?"

"But it was happening while we were shut in the drawing-room."

"So Elinor claims. But if there was anything to hide, it would have taken time. An hour or so, perhaps. You can see how Herbert would jump on that."

We went back, I remember, to speaking of the seance itself, and to the safer subject of the physical phenomena. As I have said, we did not then know of those experimenters who claim that the medium can evoke so-called rods of energy, and that by its means the invisible "controls" can perform their strange feats of levitation and the movement of solid bodies. Sperry touched very lightly on the spirit side.

"At least it would mean activity," he said. "The thought of an inert eternity is not bearable."

He was inclined, however, to believe that there were laws of which we were still in ignorance, and that we might some day find and use the fourth dimension. He seemed to be able to grasp it quite clearly. "The cube of the cube, or hypercube," he explained. "Or get it this way: a cone passed apex-downward through a plane."

"I know," I said, "that it is perfectly simple. But somehow it just sounds like words to me."

"It's perfectly clear, Horace," he insisted. "But remember this when you try to work it out; it is necessary to use motion as a translator of time into space, or of space into time."

"I don't intend to work it out," I said irritably. "But I mean to use motion as a translator of the time, which is 1:30 in the morning, to take me to a certain space, which is where I live."

But as it happened, I did not go into my house when I reached it. I was wide awake, and I perceived, on looking up at my wife's windows, that the lights were out. As it is her custom to wait up for me on those rare occasions when I spend an evening away from home, I surmised that she was comfortably asleep, and made my way to the pharmacy to which the Wellses' governess had referred.

The night-clerk was in the prescription-room behind the shop. He had fixed himself comfortably on two chairs, with an old table-cover over his knee and a half-empty bottle of sarsaparilla on a wooden box beside him. He did not waken until I spoke to him.

"Sorry to rouse you, Jim," I said.

He flung off the cover and jumped up, upsetting the bottle, which trickled a stale stream to the floor. "Oh, that's all right, Mr. Johnson, I wasn't asleep, anyhow."

I let that go, and went at once to the object of our visit. Yes, he remembered the governess, knew her, as a matter of fact. The Wellses' bought a good many things there. Asked as to her telephoning, he thought it was about nine o'clock, maybe earlier. But questioned as to what she had telephoned about, he drew himself up.

"Oh, see here," he said. "I can't very well tell you that, can I? This business has got ethics, all sorts of ethics."

He enlarged on that. The secrets of the city, he maintained loftily, were in the hands of the pharmacies. It was a trust that they kept. "Every trouble from dope to drink, and then some," he boasted.

When I told him that Arthur Wells was dead his jaw dropped, but there was no more argument in him. He knew very well the number the governess had called.

"She's done it several times," he said. "I'll be frank with you. I got curious after the third evening, and called it myself. You know the trick. I found out it was the Ellingham, house, up State Street."

"What was the nature of the conversations?"

"Oh, she was very careful. It's an open phone and any one could hear her. Once she said somebody was not to come. Another time she just said, 'This is Suzanne Gautier. 9:30, please.'"

"And tonight?"

"That the family was going out—not to call."

When I told him it was a case of suicide, his jaw dropped.

"Can you beat it?" he said. "I ask you, can you beat it? A fellow who had everything!"

But he was philosophical, too.

"A lot of people get the bug once in a while," he said. "They come in here for a dose of sudden death, and it takes watching. You'd be surprised the number of things that will do the trick if you take enough. I don't know. If things get to breaking wrong—"

His voice trailed off, and he kicked at the old table cover on the floor.

"It's a matter of the point of view," he said more cheerfully. "And my point of view just now is that this place is darned cold, and so's the street. You'd better have a little something to warm you up before you go out, Mr. Johnson."

I was chilled through, to tell the truth, and although I rarely drink anything I went back with him and took an ounce or two of villainous whiskey, poured out of a jug into a graduated glass. It is with deep humiliation of spirit I record that a housemaid coming into my library at seven o'clock the next morning, found me, in top hat and overcoat, asleep on the library couch.

I had, however, removed my collar and tie, and my watch, carefully wound, was on the smoking-stand beside me.

The death of Arthur Wells had taken place on Monday evening. Tuesday brought nothing new. The coroner was apparently satisfied, and on Wednesday the dead man's body was cremated.

"Thus obliterating all evidence," Sperry said, with what I felt was a note of relief.

But I think the situation was bothering him, and that he hoped to discount in advance the second sitting by Miss Jeremy, which Mrs. Dane had already arranged for the following Monday, for on Wednesday afternoon, following a conversation over the telephone, Sperry and I had a private sitting with Miss Jeremy in Sperry's private office. I took my wife into our confidence and invited her to be present, but the unfortunate coldness following the housemaid's discovery of me asleep in the library on the morning after the murder, was still noticeable and she refused.

The sitting, however, was totally without value. There was difficulty on the medium's part in securing the trance condition, and she broke out once rather petulantly, with the remark that we were interfering with her in some way.

I noticed that Sperry had placed Arthur Wells's stick unobtrusively on his table, but we secured only rambling and non-pertinent replies to our questions, and whether it was because I knew that outside it was broad day, or because the Wells matter did not come up at all I found a total lack of that sense of the unknown which made all the evening sittings so grisly.

I am sure she knew we had wanted something, and that she had failed to give it to us, for when she came out she was depressed and in a state of lowered vitality.

"I'm afraid I'm not helping you," she said. "I'm a little tired, I think."

She was tired. I felt suddenly very sorry for her. She was so pretty and so young—only twenty-six or thereabouts—to be in the grip of forces so relentless. Sperry sent her home in his car, and took to pacing the floor of his office.

"I'm going to give it up, Horace," he said. "Perhaps you are right. We may be on the verge of some real discovery. But while I'm interested, so interested that it interferes with my work, I'm frankly afraid to go on. There are several reasons."

I argued with him. There could be no question that if things were left as they were, a number of people would go through life convinced that Elinor Wells had murdered her husband. Look at the situation. She had sent out all the servants and the governess, surely an unusual thing in an establishment of that sort. And Miss Jeremy had been vindicated in three points; some stains had certainly been washed up, we had found the key where she had stated it to be, and Arthur had certainly been shaving himself.

"In other words," I argued, "we can't stop, Sperry. You can't stop. But my idea would be that our investigations be purely scientific and not criminal."

"Also, in other words," he said, "you think we will discover something, so you suggest that we compound a felony and keep it to ourselves!"

"Exactly," I said drily.

It is of course possible that my nerves were somewhat unstrung during the days that followed. I wakened one night to a terrific thump which shook my bed, and which seemed to be the result of some one having struck the foot-board with a plank. Immediately following this came a sharp knocking on the antique bed-warmer which hangs beside my fireplace. When I had sufficiently recovered my self-control I turned on my bedside lamp, but the room was empty.

Again I wakened with a feeling of intense cold. I was frozen with it, and curiously enough it was an inner cold. It seemed to have nothing to do with the surface of my body. I have no explanation to make of these phenomena. Like the occurrences at the seance, they were, and that was all.

But on Thursday night of that week my wife came into my bedroom, and stated flatly that there were burglars in the house.

Now it has been my contention always that if a burglar gains entrance, he should be allowed to take what he wants. Silver can be replaced, but as I said to my wife then, Horace Johnson could not. But she had recently acquired a tea set formerly belonging to her great-grandmother, and apprehension regarding it made her, for the nonce, less solicitous for me than usual.

"Either you go or I go," she said. "Where's your revolver?"

I got out of bed at that, and went down the stairs. But I must confess that I felt, the moment darkness surrounded me, considerably less trepidation concerning the possible burglar than I felt as to the darkness itself. Mrs. Johnson had locked herself in my bedroom, and there was something horrible in the black depths of the lower hall.

We are old-fashioned people, and have not yet adopted electric light. I carried a box of matches, but at the foot of the stairs the one I had lighted went out. I was terrified. I tried to light another match, but there was a draft from somewhere, and it too was extinguished before I had had time to glance about. I was immediately conscious of a sort of soft movement around me, as of shadowy shapes that passed and repassed. Once it seemed to me that a hand was laid on my shoulder and was not lifted, but instead dissolved into the other shadows around. The sudden striking of the clock on the stair landing completed my demoralization. I turned and fled upstairs, pursued, to my agonized nerves, by ghostly hands that came toward me from between the spindles of the stair-rail.

At dawn I went downstairs again, heartily ashamed of myself. I found that a door to the basement had been left open, and that the soft movement had probably been my overcoat, swaying in the draft.

Probably. I was not certain. Indeed, I was certain of nothing during those strange days. I had built up for myself a universe upheld by certain laws, of day and night, of food and sleep and movement, of three dimensions of space. And now, it seemed to me, I had stood all my life but on the threshold, and, for an hour or so, the door had opened.

Sperry had, I believe, told Herbert Robinson of what we had discovered, but nothing had been said to the women. I knew through my wife that they were wildly curious, and the night of the second seance Mrs. Dane drew me aside and I saw that she suspected, without knowing, that we had been endeavoring to check up our revelations with the facts.

"I want you to promise me one thing," she said. "I'll not bother you now. But I'm an old woman, with not much more of life to be influenced by any disclosures. When this thing is over, and you have come to a conclusion—I'll not put it that way: you may not come to a conclusion—but when it is over, I want you to tell me the whole story. Will you?"

I promised that I would.

Miss Jeremy did not come to dinner. She never ate before a seance. And although we tried to keep the conversational ball floating airily, there was not the usual effervescence of the Neighborhood Club dinners. One and all, we were waiting, we knew not for what.

I am sorry to record that there were no physical phenomena of any sort at this second seance. The room was arranged as it had been at the first sitting, except that a table with a candle and a chair had been placed behind a screen for Mrs. Dane's secretary.

There was one other change. Sperry had brought the walking-stick he had taken from Arthur Wells's room, and after the medium was in trance he placed it on the table before her.

The first questions were disappointing in results. Asked about the stick, there was only silence. When, however, Sperry went back to the sitting of the week before, and referred to questions and answers at that time, the medium seemed uneasy. Her hand, held under mine, made an effort to free itself and, released, touched the cane. She lifted it, and struck the table a hard blow with it.

"Do you know to whom that stick belongs?"

A silence. Then: "Yes."

"Will you tell us what you know about it?"

"It is writing."

"Writing?"

"It was writing, but the water washed it away."

Then, instantly and with great rapidity, followed a wild torrent of words and incomplete sentences. It is inarticulate, and the secretary made no record of it. As I recall, however, it was about water, children, and the words "ten o'clock" repeated several times.

"Do you mean that something happened at ten o'clock?"

"No. Certainly not. No, indeed. The water washed it away. All of it. Not a trace."

"Where did all this happen?"

She named, without hesitation, a seaside resort about fifty miles from our city. There was not one of us, I dare say, who did not know that the Wellses had spent the preceding summer there and that Charlie Ellingham had been there, also.

"Do you know that Arthur Wells is dead?"

"Yes. He is dead."

"Did he kill himself?"

"You can't catch me on that. I don't know."

Here the medium laughed. It was horrible. And the laughter made the whole thing absurd. But it died away quickly.

"If only the pocketbook was not lost," she said. "There were so many things in it. Especially car-tickets. Walking is a nuisance."

Mrs. Dane's secretary suddenly spoke. "Do you want me to take things like that?" she asked.

"Take everything, please," was the answer.

"Car-tickets and letters. It will be terrible if the letters are found."

"Where was the pocketbook lost?" Sperry asked.

"If that were known, it could be found," was the reply, rather sharply given. "Hawkins may have it. He was always hanging around. The curtain was much safer."

"What curtain?"

"Nobody would have thought of the curtain. First ideas are best."

She repeated this, following it, as once before, with rhymes for the final word, best, rest, chest, pest.

"Pest!" she said. "That's Hawkins!" And again the laughter.

"Did one of the bullets strike the ceiling?"

"Yes. But you'll never find it. It is holding well. That part's safe enough—unless it made a hole in the floor above."

"But there was only one empty chamber in the revolver. How could two shots have been fired?"

There was no answer at all to this. And Sperry, after waiting, went on to his next question: "Who occupied the room overhead?"

But here we received the reply to the previous question: "There was a box of cartridges in the table-drawer. That's easy."

From that point, however, the interest lapsed. Either there was no answer to questions, or we got the absurdity that we had encountered before, about the drawing-room furniture. But, unsatisfactory in many ways as the seance had been, the effect on Miss Jeremy was profound—she was longer in coming out, and greatly exhausted when it was all over.

She refused to take the supper Mrs. Dane had prepared for her, and at eleven o'clock Sperry took her home in his car.

I remember that Mrs. Dane inquired, after she had gone.

"Does any one know the name of the Wellses' butler? Is it Hawkins?"

I said nothing, and as Sperry was the only one likely to know and he had gone, the inquiry went no further. Looking back, I realize that Herbert, while less cynical, was still skeptical, that his sister was non-committal, but for some reason watching me, and that Mrs. Dane was in a state of delightful anticipation.

My wife, however, had taken a dislike to Miss Jeremy, and said that the whole thing bored her.

"The men like it, of course," she said, "Horace fairly simpers with pleasure while he sits and holds her hand. But a woman doesn't impose on other women so easily. It's silly."

"My dear," Mrs. Dane said, reaching over and patting my wife's hand, "people talked that way about Columbus and Galileo. And if it is nonsense it is such thrilling nonsense!"

VI

I find that the solution of the Arthur Wells mystery—for we did solve it—takes three divisions in my mind. Each one is a sitting, followed by an investigation made by Sperry and myself.

But for some reason, after Miss Jeremy's second sitting, I found that my reasoning mind was stronger than my credulity. And as Sperry had at that time determined to have nothing more to do with the business, I made a resolution to abandon my investigations. Nor have I any reason to believe that I would have altered my attitude toward the case, had it not been that I saw in the morning paper on the Thursday following the second seance, that Elinor Wells had closed her house, and gone to Florida.

I tried to put the fact out of my mind that morning. After all, what good would it do? No discovery of mine could bring Arthur Wells back to his family, to his seat at the bridge table at the club, to his too expensive cars and his unpaid bills. Or to his wife who was not grieving for him.

On the other hand, I confess to an overwhelming desire to examine again the ceiling of the dressing room and thus to check up one degree further the accuracy of our revelations. After some debate, therefore, I called up Sperry, but he flatly refused to go on any further.

"Miss Jeremy has been ill since Monday," he said. "Mrs. Dane's rheumatism is worse, her companion is nervously upset, and your own wife called me up an hour ago and says you are sleeping with a light, and she thinks you ought to go away. The whole club is shot to pieces."

But, although I am a small and not a courageous man, the desire to examine the Wells house clung to me tenaciously. Suppose there were cartridges in his table drawer? Suppose I should find the second bullet hole in the ceiling? I no longer deceived myself by any argument that my interest was purely scientific. There is a point at which curiosity becomes unbearable, when it becomes an obsession, like hunger. I had reached that point.

Nevertheless, I found it hard to plan the necessary deception to my wife. My habits have always been entirely orderly and regular. My wildest dissipation was the Neighborhood Club. I could not recall an evening away from home in years, except on business. Yet now I must have a free evening, possibly an entire night.

In planning for this, I forgot my nervousness for a time. I decided finally to tell my wife that an out-of-town client wished to talk business with me, and that day, at luncheon—I go home to luncheon—I mentioned that such a client was in town.

"It is possible," I said, as easily as I could, "that we may not get through this afternoon. If things should run over into the evening, I'll telephone."

She took it calmly enough, but later on, as I was taking an electric flash from the drawer of the hall table and putting it in my overcoat pocket, she came on me, and I thought she looked surprised.

During the afternoon I was beset with doubts and uneasiness. Suppose she called up my office and found that the client I had named was not in town? It is undoubtedly true that a tangled web we weave when first we practise to deceive, for on my return to the office I was at once quite certain that Mrs. Johnson would telephone and make the inquiry.

After some debate I called my secretary and told her to say, if such a message came in, that Mr. Forbes was in town and that I had an appointment with him. As a matter of fact, no such inquiry came in, but as Miss Joyce, my secretary, knew that Mr. Forbes was in Europe, I was conscious for some months afterwards that Miss Joyce's eyes occasionally rested on me in a speculative and suspicious manner.

Other things also increased my uneasiness as the day wore on. There was, for instance, the matter of the back door to the Wells house. Nothing was more unlikely than that the key would still be hanging there. I must, therefore, get a key.

At three o'clock I sent the office-boy out for a back-door key. He looked so surprised that I explained that we had lost our key, and that I required an assortment of keys of all sizes.

"What sort of key?" he demanded, eyeing me, with his feet apart.

"Just an ordinary key," I said. "Not a Yale key. Nothing fancy. Just a plain back-door key." At something after four my wife called up, in great excitement. A boy and a man had been to the house and had fitted an extra key to the back door, which had two excellent ones already. She was quite hysterical, and had sent for the police, but the officer had arrived after they had gone.

"They are burglars, of course!" she said. "Burglars often have boys with them, to go through the pantry windows. I'm so nervous I could scream."

I tried to tell her that if the door was unlocked there was no need to use the pantry window, but she rang off quickly and, I thought, coldly. Not, however, before she had said that my plan to spend the evening out was evidently known in the underworld!

By going through my desk I found a number of keys, mostly trunk keys and one the key to a dog-collar. But late in the afternoon I visited a client of mine who is in the hardware business, and secured quite a selection. One of them was a skeleton key. He persisted in regarding the matter as a joke, and poked me between the shoulder-blades as I went out.

"If you're arrested with all that hardware on you," he said, "you'll be held as a first-class burglar. You are equipped to open anything from a can of tomatoes to the missionary box in church."

But I felt that already, innocent as I was, I was leaving a trail of suspicion behind me: Miss Joyce and the office boy, the dealer and my wife. And I had not started yet.

I dined in a small chop-house where I occasionally lunch, and took a large cup of strong black coffee. When I went out into the night again I found that a heavy fog had settled down, and I began to feel again something of the strange and disturbing quality of the day which had ended in Arthur Wells's death. Already a potential housebreaker, I avoided policemen, and the very jingling of the keys in my pocket sounded loud and incriminating to my ears.

The Wells house was dark. Even the arc-lamp in the street was shrouded in fog. But the darkness, which added to my nervousness, added also to my security.

I turned and felt my way cautiously to the rear of the house. Suddenly I remembered the dog. But of course he was gone. As I cautiously ascended the steps the dead leaves on the vines rattled, as at the light touch of a hand, and I was tempted to turn and run.

I do not like deserted houses. Even in daylight they have a sinister effect on me. They seem, in their empty spaces, to have held and recorded all that has happened in the dusty past. The Wells house that night, looming before me, silent and mysterious, seemed the embodiment of all the deserted houses I had known. Its empty and unshuttered windows were like blind eyes, gazing in, not out.

Nevertheless, now that the time had come a certain amount of courage came with it. I am not ashamed to confess that a certain part of it came from the anticipation of the Neighborhood Club's plaudits. For Herbert to have made such an investigation, or even Sperry, with his height and his iron muscles, would not have surprised them. But I was aware that while they expected intelligence and even humor, of a sort, from me, they did not anticipate any particular bravery.

The flash was working, but rather feebly. I found the nail where the door-key had formerly hung, but the key, as I had expected, was gone. I was less than five minutes, I fancy, in finding a key from my collection that would fit. The bolt slid back with a click, and the door opened.

It was still early in the evening, eight-thirty or thereabouts. I tried to think of that; to remember that, only a few blocks away, some of my friends were still dining, or making their way into theaters. But the silence of the house came out to meet me on the threshold, and its blackness enveloped me like a wave. It was unfortunate, too, that I remembered just then that it was, or soon would be, the very hour of young Wells's death.

Nevertheless, once inside the house, the door to the outside closed and facing two alternatives, to go on with it or to cut and run, I found a sort of desperate courage, clenched my teeth, and felt for the nearest light switch.

The electric light had been cut off!

I should have expected it, but I had not. I remember standing in the back hall and debating whether to go on or to get out. I was not only in a highly nervous state, but I was also badly handicapped.

However, as the moments wore on and I stood there, with the quiet unbroken by no mysterious sounds, I gained a certain confidence. After a short period of readjustment, therefore, I felt my way to the library door, and into the room. Once there, I used the flash to discover that the windows were shuttered, and proceeded to take off my hat and coat, which I placed on a chair near the door. It was at this time that I discovered that the battery of my lamp was very weak, and finding a candle in a tall brass stick on the mantelpiece, I lighted it.

Then I looked about. The house had evidently been hastily closed. Some of the furniture was covered with sheets, while part of it stood unprotected. The rug had been folded into the center of the room, and covered with heavy brown papers, and I was extremely startled to hear the papers rustling. A mouse, however, proved to be the source of the sound, and I pulled myself together with a jerk.

It is to be remembered that I had left my hat and overcoat on a chair near the door. There could be no mistake, as the chair was a light one, and the weight of my overcoat threw it back against the wall.

Candle in hand, I stepped out into the hall, and was immediately met by a crash which reverberated through the house. In my alarm my teeth closed on the end of my tongue, with agonizing results, but the sound died away, and I concluded that an upper window had been left open, and that the rising wind had slammed a door. But my morale, as we say since the war, had been shaken, and I recklessly lighted a second candle and placed it on the table in the hall at the foot of the staircase, to facilitate my exit in case I desired to make a hurried one.

Then I climbed slowly. The fog had apparently made its way into the house, for when, halfway up, I turned and looked down, the candlelight was hardly more than a spark, surrounded by a luminous aura.

I do not know exactly when I began to feel that I was not alone in the house. It was, I think, when I was on a chair on top of a table in Arthur's room, with my candle upheld to the ceiling. It seemed to me that something was moving stealthily in the room overhead. I stood there, candle upheld, and every faculty I possessed seemed centered in my ears. It was not a footstep. It was a soft and dragging movement. Had I not been near the ceiling I should not have heard it. Indeed, a moment later I was not certain that I had heard it.

My chair, on top of the table, was none too securely balanced. I had found what I was looking for, a part of the plaster ornament broken away, and replaced by a whitish substance, not plaster. I got out my penknife and cut away the foreign matter, showing a small hole beneath, a bullet-hole, if I knew anything about bullet-holes.

Then I heard the dragging movement above, and what with alarm and my insecure position, I suddenly overbalanced, chair and all. My head must have struck on the corner of the table, for I was dazed for a few moments. The candle had gone out, of course. I felt for the chair, righted it, and sat down. I was dizzy and I was frightened. I was afraid to move, lest the dragging thing above come down and creep over me in the darkness and smother me.

And sitting there, I remembered the very things I most wished to forget—the black curtain behind Miss Jeremy, the things flung by unseen hands into the room, the way my watch had slid over the table and fallen to the floor.

Since that time I know there is a madness of courage, born of terror. Nothing could be more intolerable than to sit there and wait. It is the same insanity that drove men out of the trenches to the charge and almost certain death, rather than to sit and wait for what might come.

In a way, I daresay I charged the upper floor of the house. Recalling the situation from this safe lapse of time, I think that I was in a condition close to frenzy. I know that it did not occur to me to leap down the staircase and escape, and I believe now this was due to a conviction that I was dealing with the supernatural, and that on no account did I dare to turn my back on it. All children and some adults, I am sure, have known this feeling.

Whatever drove me, I know that, candle in hand, and hardly sane, I ran up the staircase, and into the room overhead. It was empty.

As suddenly as my sanity had gone, it returned to me. The sight of two small beds, side by side, a tiny dressing-table, a row of toys on the mantelpiece, was calming. Here was the children's night nursery, a white and placid room which could house nothing hideous.

I was humiliated and ashamed. I, Horace Johnson, a man of dignity and reputation, even in a small way, a successful after-dinner speaker, numbering fifty-odd years of logical living to my credit, had been running half-maddened toward a mythical danger from which I had been afraid to run away!

I sat down and mopped my face with my pocket handkerchief.

After a time I got up, and going to a window looked down at the quiet world below. The fog was lifting. Automobiles were making cautious progress along the slippery street. A woman with a basket had stopped under the street light and was rearranging her parcels. The clock of the city hall, visible over the opposite roofs, marked only twenty minutes to nine. It was still early evening—not even midnight, the magic hour of the night.

Somehow that fact reassured me, and I was able to take stock of my surroundings. I realized, for instance, that I stood in the room over Arthur's dressing room, and that it was into the ceiling under me that the second—or probably the first—bullet had penetrated. I know, as it happens, very little of firearms, but I did realize that a shot from a .45 Colt automatic would have considerable penetrative power. To be exact, that the bullet had probably either lodged itself in a joist, or had penetrated through the flooring and might be somewhere over my head.

But my candle was inadequate for more than the most superficial examination of the ceiling, which presented so far as I could see an unbroken surface. I turned my attention, therefore, to the floor. It was when I was turning the rug back that I recognized the natural and not supernatural origin of the sound which had so startled me. It had been the soft movement of the carpet across the floor boards.

Some one, then, had been there before me—some one who knew what I knew, had reasoned as I reasoned. Some one who, in all probability, still lurked on the upper floor.

Obeying an impulse, I stood erect and called out sharply, "Sperry!" I said. "Sperry!"

There was no answer. I tried again, calling Herbert. But only my own voice came back to me, and the whistling of the wind through the window I had opened.

My fears, never long in abeyance that night, roused again. I had instantly a conviction that some human figure, sinister and dangerous, was lurking in the shadows of that empty floor, and I remember backing away from the door and standing in the center of the room, prepared for some stealthy, murderous assault. When none came I looked about for a weapon, and finally took the only thing in sight, a coal-tongs from the fireplace. Armed with that, I made a cursory round of the near-by rooms but there was no one hiding in them.

I went back to the rug and examined the floor beneath it. I was right. Some one had been there before me. Bits of splintered wood lay about. The second bullet had been fired, had buried itself in the flooring, and had, some five minutes before, been dug out.

VII

The extraordinary thing about the Arthur Wells story was not his killing. For killing it was. It was the way it was solved.

Here was a young woman, Miss Jeremy, who had not known young Wells, had not known his wife, had, until that first meeting at Mrs. Dane's, never met any member of the Neighborhood Club. Yet, but for her, Arthur Wells would have gone to his grave bearing the stigma of moral cowardice, of suicide.

The solution, when it came, was amazing, but remarkably simple. Like most mysteries. I have in my own house, for instance, an example of a great mystery, founded on mere absentmindedness.

This is what my wife terms the mystery of the fire-tongs.

I had left the Wells house as soon as I had made the discovery in the night nursery. I carried the candle and the fire-tongs downstairs. I was, apparently, calm but watchful. I would have said that I had never been more calm in my life. I knew quite well that I had the fire-tongs in my hand. Just when I ceased to be cognizant of them was probably when, on entering the library, I found that my overcoat had disappeared, and that my stiff hat, badly broken, lay on the floor. However, as I say, I was still extraordinarily composed. I picked up my hat, and moving to the rear door, went out and closed it. When I reached the street, however, I had only gone a few yards when I discovered that I was still carrying the lighted candle, and that a man, passing by, had stopped and was staring after me.

My composure is shown by the fact that I dropped the candle down the next sewer opening, but the fact remains that I carried the fire-tongs home. I do not recall doing so. In fact, I knew nothing of the matter until morning. On the way to my house I was elaborating a story to the effect that my overcoat had been stolen from a restaurant where I and my client had dined. The hat offered more serious difficulties. I fancied that, by kissing my wife good-by at the breakfast table, I might be able to get out without her following me to the front door, which is her custom.

But, as a matter of fact, I need not have concerned myself about the hat. When I descended to breakfast the next morning I found her surveying the umbrella-stand in the hall. The fire-tongs were standing there, gleaming, among my sticks and umbrellas.

I lied. I lied shamelessly. She is a nervous woman, and, as we have no children, her attitude toward me is one of watchful waiting. Through long years she has expected me to commit some indiscretion—innocent, of course, such as going out without my overcoat on a cool day—and she intends to be on hand for every emergency. I dared not confess, therefore, that on the previous evening I had burglariously entered a closed house, had there surprised another intruder at work, had fallen and bumped my head severely, and had, finally, had my overcoat taken.

"Horace," she said coldly, "where did you get those fire-tongs?"

"Fire-tongs?" I repeated. "Why, that's so. They are fire-tongs."

"Where did you get them?"

"My dear," I expostulated, "I get them?"

"What I would like to ask," she said, with an icy calmness that I have learned to dread, "is whether you carried them home over your head, under the impression that you had your umbrella."

"Certainly not," I said with dignity. "I assure you, my dear—"

"I am not a curious woman," she put in incisively, "but when my husband spends an evening out, and returns minus his overcoat, with his hat mashed, a lump the size of an egg over his ear, and puts a pair of fire-tongs in the umbrella stand under the impression that it is an umbrella, I have a right to ask at least if he intends to continue his life of debauchery."

I made a mistake then. I should have told her. Instead, I took my broken hat and jammed it on my head with a force that made the lump she had noticed jump like a toothache, and went out.

When, at noon and luncheon, I tried to tell her the truth, she listened to the end: Then: "I should think you could have done better than that," she said. "You have had all morning to think it out."

However, if things were in a state of armed neutrality at home, I had a certain compensation for them when I told my story to Sperry that afternoon.

"You see how it is," I finished. "You can stay out of this, or come in, Sperry, but I cannot stop now. He was murdered beyond a doubt, and there is an intelligent effort being made to eliminate every particle of evidence."

He nodded.

"It looks like it. And this man who was there last night—"

"Why a man?"

"He took your overcoat, instead of his own, didn't he? It may have been—it's curious, isn't it, that we've had no suggestion of Ellingham in all the rest of the material."

Like the other members of the Neighborhood Club, he had a copy of the proceedings at the two seances, and now he brought them out and fell to studying them.

"She was right about the bullet in the ceiling," he reflected. "I suppose you didn't look for the box of shells for the revolver?"

"I meant to, but it slipped my mind."

He shuffled the loose pages of the record. "Cane—washed away by the water—a knee that is hurt—the curtain would have been safer —Hawkins—the drawing-room furniture is all over the house. That last, Horace, isn't pertinent. It refers clearly to the room we were in. Of course, the point is, how much of the rest is also extraneous matter?" He re-read one of the sheets. "Of course that belongs, about Hawkins. And probably this: 'It will be terrible if the letters are found.' They were in the pocketbook, presumably."

He folded up the papers and replaced them in a drawer.

"We'd better go back to the house," he said. "Whoever took your overcoat by mistake probably left one. The difficulty is, of course, that he probably discovered his error and went back again last night. Confound it, man, if you had thought of that at the time, we would have something to go on today."

"If I had thought of a number of things I'd have stayed out of the place altogether," I retorted tartly. "I wish you could help me about the fire-tongs, Sperry. I don't seem able to think of any explanation that Mrs. Johnson would be willing to accept."

"Tell her the truth."

"I don't think you understand," I explained. "She simply wouldn't believe it. And if she did I should have to agree to drop the investigation. As a matter of fact, Sperry, I had resorted to subterfuge in order to remain out last evening, and I am bitterly regretting my mendacity."

But Sperry has, I am afraid, rather loose ideas.

"Every man," he said, "would rather tell the truth, but every woman makes it necessary to lie to her. Forget the fire-tongs, Horace, and forget Mrs. Johnson to-night. He may not have dared to go back in day-light for his overcoat."

"Very well," I agreed.

But it was not very well, and I knew it. I felt that, in a way, my whole domestic happiness was at stake. My wife is a difficult person to argue with, and as tenacious of an opinion once formed as are all very amiable people. However, unfortunately for our investigation, but luckily for me, under the circumstances, Sperry was called to another city that afternoon and did not return for two days.

It was, it will be recalled, on the Thursday night following the second sitting that I had gone alone to the Wells house, and my interview with Sperry was on Friday. It was on Friday afternoon that I received a telephone message from Mrs. Dane.

It was actually from her secretary, the Clara who had recorded the seances. It was Mrs. Dane's misfortune to be almost entirely dependent on the various young women who, one after the other, were employed to look after her. I say "one after the other" advisedly. It had long been a matter of good-natured jesting in the Neighborhood Club that Mrs. Dane conducted a matrimonial bureau, as one young woman after another was married from her house. It was her kindly habit, on such occasions, to give the bride a wedding, and only a month before it had been my privilege to give away in holy wedlock Miss Clara's predecessor.

"Mrs. Dane would like you to stop in and have a cup of tea with her this afternoon, Mr. Johnson," said the secretary.

"At what time?"

"At four o'clock."

I hesitated. I felt that my wife was waiting at home for further explanation of the coal-tongs, and that the sooner we had it out the better. But, on the other hand, Mrs. Dane's invitations, by reason of her infirmity, took on something of the nature of commands.

"Please say that I will be there at four," I replied.

I bought a new hat that afternoon, and told the clerk to destroy the old one. Then I went to Mrs. Dane's.

She was in the drawing-room, now restored to its usual clutter of furniture and ornaments. I made my way around two tables, stepped over a hassock and under the leaves of an artificial palm, and shook her hand.

She was plainly excited. Never have I known a woman who, confined to a wheel-chair, lived so hard. She did not allow life to pass her windows, if I may put it that way. She called it in, and set it moving about her chair, herself the nucleus around which were enacted all sorts of small neighborhood dramas and romances. Her secretaries did not marry. She married them.

It is curious to look back and remember how Herbert and Sperry and myself had ignored this quality in her, in the Wells case. She was not to be ignored, as I discovered that afternoon.

"Sit down," she said. "You look half sick, Horace."

Nothing escapes her eyes, so I was careful to place myself with the lump on my head turned away from her. But I fancy she saw it, for her eyes twinkled.

"Horace! Horace!" she said. "How I have detested you all week!"

"I? You detested me?"

"Loathed you," she said with unction. "You are cruel and ungrateful. Herbert has influenza, and does not count. And Sperry is in love—oh yes, I know it. I know a great many things. But you!"

I could only stare at her.

"The strange thing is," she went on, "that I have known you for years, and never suspected your sense of humor. You'll forgive me, I know, if I tell you that your lack of humor was to my mind the only flaw in an otherwise perfect character."

"I am not aware—" I began stiffly. "I have always believed that I furnished to the Neighborhood Club its only leaven of humor."

"Don't spoil it," she begged. "Don't. If you could know how I have enjoyed it. All afternoon I have been chuckling. The fire-tongs, Horace. The fire-tongs!"

Then I knew that my wife had been to Mrs. Dane and I drew a long breath. "I assure you," I said gravely, "that while doubtless I carried the wretched things home and—er—placed them where they were found, I have not the slightest recollection of it. And it is hardly amusing, is it?"

"Amusing!" she cried. "It's delicious. It has made me a young woman again. Horace, if I could have seen your wife's face when she found them, I would give cheerfully almost anything I possess."

But underneath her mirth I knew there was something else. And, after all, she could convince my wife if she were convinced herself. I told the whole story—of the visit Sperry and I had made the night Arthur Wells was shot, and of what we discovered; of the clerk at the pharmacy and his statement, and even of the whiskey and its unfortunate effect—at which, I regret to say, she was vastly amused; and, last of all, of my experience the previous night in the deserted house.

She was very serious when I finished. Tea came, but we forgot to drink it. Her eyes flashed with excitement, her faded face flushed. And, with it all, as I look back, there was an air of suppressed excitement that seemed to have nothing to do with my narrative. I remembered it, however, when the denouement came the following week.

She was a remarkable woman. Even then she knew, or strongly suspected, the thing that the rest of us had missed, the x of the equation. But I think it only fair to record that she was in possession of facts which we did not have, and which she did not divulge until the end.

"You have been so ungenerous with me," she said finally, "that I am tempted not to tell you why I sent for you. Of course, I know I am only a helpless old woman, and you men are people of affairs. But now and then I have a flash of intelligence. I'm going to tell you, but you don't deserve it."

She went down into the black silk bag at her side which was as much a part of her attire as the false front she wore with such careless abandon, and which, brown in color and indifferently waved, was invariably parting from its mooring. She drew out a newspaper clipping.

"On going over Clara's notes," she said, "I came to the conclusion, last Tuesday, that the matter of the missing handbag and the letters was important. More important, probably, than the mere record shows. Do you recall the note of distress in Miss Jeremy's voice? It was almost a wail."

I had noticed it.

"I have plenty of time to think," she added, not without pathos. "There is only one Monday night in the week, and—the days are long. It occurred to me to try to trace that bag."

"In what way?"

"How does any one trace lost articles?" she demanded. "By advertising, of course. Last Wednesday I advertised for the bag."

I was too astonished to speak.

"I reasoned like this: If there was no such bag, there was no harm done. As a matter of fact, if there was no such bag, the chances were that we were all wrong, anyhow. If there was such a bag, I wanted it. Here is the advertisement as I inserted it."

She gave me a small newspaper cutting

"Lost, a handbag containing private letters, car-tickets, etc. Liberal reward paid for its return. Please write to A 31, the Daily News."

I sat with it on my palm. It was so simple, so direct. And I, a lawyer, and presumably reasonably acute, had not thought of it!

"You are wasted on us, Mrs. Dane," I acknowledged. "Well? I see something has come of it."

"Yes, but I'm not ready for it."

She dived again into the bag, and brought up another clipping.

"On the day that I had that inserted," she said impressively, "this also appeared. They were in the same column." She read the second clipping aloud, slowly, that I might gain all its significance:

"Lost on the night of Monday, November the second, between State Avenue and Park Avenue, possibly on an Eastern Line street car, a black handbag containing keys, car-tickets, private letters, and a small sum of money. Reward and no questions asked if returned to Daily News office."

She passed the clipping to me and I compared the two. It looked strange, and I confess to a tingling feeling that coincidence, that element so much to be feared in any investigation, was not the solution here. But there was such a chance, and I spoke of it.

"Coincidence rubbish!" she retorted. "I am not through, my friend."

She went down into the bag again, and I expected nothing less than the pocketbook, letters and all, to appear. But she dragged up, among a miscellany of handkerchiefs, a bottle of smelling-salts, and a few almonds, of which she was inordinately fond, an envelope.

"Yesterday," she said, "I took a taxicab ride. You know my chair gets tiresome, occasionally. I stopped at the newspaper office, and found the bag had not been turned in, but that there was a letter for A 31." She held out the envelope to me.

"Read it," she observed. "It is a curious human document. You'll probably be no wiser for reading it, but it shows one thing: We are on the track of something."

I have the letter before me now. It is written on glazed paper, ruled with blue lines. The writing is of the flowing style we used to call Spencerian, and if it lacks character I am inclined to believe that its weakness is merely the result of infrequent use of a pen.

You know who this is from. I have the bag and the letters. In a safe place. If you would treat me like a human being, you could have them. I know where the walking-stick is, also. I will tell you this. I have no wish to do her any harm. She will have to pay up in the next world, even if she gets off in this. The way I reason is this: As long as I have the things, I've got the whiphand. I've got you, too, although you may think I haven't.

About the other matter I was innocent. I swear it again. I never did it. You are the only one in all the world. I would rather be dead than go on like this.

It is unsigned.

I stared from the letter to Mrs. Dane. She was watching me, her face grave and rather sad.

"You and I, Horace," she said, "live our orderly lives. We eat, and sleep, and talk, and even labor. We think we are living. But for the last day or two I have been seeing visions—you and I and the rest of us, living on the surface, and underneath, carefully kept down so it will not make us uncomfortable, a world of passion and crime and violence and suffering. That letter is a tragedy."

But if she had any suspicion then as to the writer, and I think she had not, she said nothing, and soon after I started for home. I knew that one of two things would have happened there: either my wife would have put away the fire-tongs, which would indicate a truce, or they would remain as they had been, which would indicate that she still waited for the explanation I could not give. It was with a certain tension, therefore, that I opened my front door.

The fire-tongs still stood in the stand.

In one way, however, Mrs. Johnson's refusal to speak to me that evening had a certain value, for it enabled me to leave the house without explanation, and thus to discover that, if an overcoat had been left in place of my own, it had been taken away. It also gave me an opportunity to return the fire-tongs, a proceeding which I had considered would assist in a return of the entente cordiale at home, but which most unjustly appeared to have exactly the opposite effect. It has been my experience that the most innocent action may, under certain circumstances, assume an appearance of extreme guilt.

By Saturday the condition of affairs between my wife and myself remained in statu quo, and I had decided on a bold step. This was to call a special meeting of the Neighborhood Club, without Miss Jeremy, and put before them the situation as it stood at that time, with a view to formulating a future course of action, and also of publicly vindicating myself before my wife.

In deference to Herbert Robinson's recent attack of influenza, we met at the Robinson house. Sperry himself wheeled Mrs. Dane over, and made a speech.

"We have called this meeting," he said, "because a rather singular situation has developed. What was commenced purely as an interesting experiment has gone beyond that stage. We find ourselves in the curious position of taking what comes very close to being a part in a domestic tragedy. The affair is made more delicate by the fact that this tragedy involves people who, if not our friends, at least are very well known to us. The purpose of this meeting, to be brief, is to determine whether the Neighborhood Club, as a body, wishes to go on with the investigation, or to stop where we are."

He paused, but, as no one spoke, he went on again. "It is really not as simple as that," he said. "To stop now, in view of the evidence we intend to place before the Club, is to leave in all our minds certain suspicions that may be entirely unjust. On the other hand, to go on is very possible to place us all in a position where to keep silent is to be an accessory after a crime."

He then proceeded, in orderly fashion, to review the first sitting and its results. He read from notes, elaborating them as he went along, for the benefit of the women, who had not been fully informed. As all the data of the Club is now in my possession, I copy these notes.

"I shall review briefly the first sitting, and what followed it." He read the notes of the sitting first. "You will notice that I have made no comment on the physical phenomena which occurred early in the seance. This is for two reasons: first, it has no bearing on the question at issue. Second, it has no quality of novelty. Certain people, under certain conditions, are able to exert powers that we can not explain. I have no belief whatever in their spiritistic quality. They are purely physical, the exercise of powers we have either not yet risen high enough in our scale of development to recognize generally, or which have survived from some early period when our natural gifts had not been smothered by civilization."

And, to make our position clear, that is today the attitude of the Neighborhood Club. The supernormal, as I said at the beginning, not the supernatural, is our explanation.

Sperry's notes were alphabetical.

a At 9:15, or somewhat earlier, on Monday night a week ago Arthur Wells killed himself, or was killed. At 9:30 on that same evening by Mr. Johnson's watch, consulted at the time, Miss Jeremy had described such a crime. Here he elaborated, repeating the medium's account.

b At midnight, Sperry, reaching home, had found a message summoning him to the Wells house. The message had been left at 9:35. He had telephoned me, and we had gone together, arriving at approximately 12:30.

c We had been unable to enter, and, recalling the medium's description of a key on a nail among the vines, had searched for and found such a key, and had admitted ourselves. Mrs. Wells, a governess, a doctor, and two policemen were in the house. The dead man lay in the room in which he had died. Here he went at length into the condition of the room, the revolver with one chamber empty, and the blood-stained sponge and razorstrop behind the bathtub. We had made a hasty examination of the ceiling, but had found no trace of a second shot.

d The governess had come in at just after the death. Mr. Horace Johnson had had a talk with her. She had left the front door unfastened when she went out at eight o'clock. She said she had gone out to telephone about another position, as she was dissatisfied. She had phoned from, Elliott's pharmacy on State Avenue. Later that night Mr. Johnson had gone to Elliott's. She had lied about the message. She had really telephoned to a number which the pharmacy clerk had already discovered was that of the Ellingham house. The message was that Mr. Ellingham was not to come, as Mr. and Mrs. Wells were going out. It was not the first time she had telephoned to that number.

There was a stir in the room. Something which we had tacitly avoided had come suddenly into the open. Sperry raised his hand.

"It is necessary to be explicit," he said, "that the Club may see where it stands. It is, of course, not necessary to remind ourselves that this evening's disclosures are of the most secret nature. I urge that the Club jump to no hasty conclusions, and that there shall be no interruptions until we have finished with our records."

e At a private seance, which Mr. Johnson and I decided was excusable under the circumstances, the medium was unable to give us anything. This in spite of the fact that we had taken with us a walking-stick belonging to the dead man.

f The second sitting of the Club. I need only refresh your minds as to one or two things; the medium spoke of a lost pocketbook, and of letters. While the point is at least capable of doubt, apparently the letters were in the pocketbook. Also, she said that a curtain would have been better, that Hawkins was a nuisance, and that everything was all right unless the bullet had made a hole in the floor above. You will also recall the mention of a box of cartridges in a table drawer in Arthur Wells's room.

"I will now ask Mr. Horace Johnson to tell what occurred on the night before last, Thursday evening."

"I do not think Horace has a very clear recollection of last Thursday night," my wife said, coldly. "And I wish to go on record at once that if he claims that spirits broke his hat, stole his overcoat, bumped his head and sent him home with a pair of fire-tongs for a walking-stick, I don't believe him."

Which attitude Herbert, I regret to say, did not help when he said:

"Don't worry, Horace will soon be too old for the gay life. Remember your arteries, Horace."

I have quoted this interruption to show how little, outside of Sperry, Mrs. Dane and myself, the Neighborhood Club appreciated the seriousness of the situation. Herbert, for instance, had been greatly amused when Sperry spoke of my finding the razorstrop and had almost chuckled over our investigation of the ceiling.

But they were very serious when I had finished my statement.

"Great Scott!" Herbert said. "Then she was right, after all! I say, I guess I've been no end of an ass."

I was inclined to agree with him. But the real effect of my brief speech was on my wife.

It was a real compensation for that night of terror and for the uncomfortable time since to find her gaze no longer cold, but sympathetic, and—if I may be allowed to say so—admiring. When at last I sat down beside her, she put her hand on my arm in a way that I had missed since the unfortunate affair of the pharmacy whiskey.

Mrs. Dane then read and explained the two clippings and the letter, and the situation, so far as it had developed, was before the Club.

Were we to go on, or to stop?

Put to a vote, the women were for going on. The men were more doubtful, and Herbert voiced what I think we all felt.

"We're getting in pretty deep," he said. "We have no right to step in where the law has stepped out—no legal right, that is. As to moral right, it depends on what we are holding these sittings for. If we are making what we started out to make, an investigation into psychic matters, then we can go on. But with this proviso, I think: Whatever may come of it, the result is of psychic interest only. We are not trailing a criminal."

"Crime is the affair of every decent-minded citizen," his sister put in concisely.

But the general view was that Herbert was right. I am not defending our course. I am recording it. It is, I admit, open to argument.

Having decided on what to do, or not to do, we broke into animated discussion. The letter to A 31 was the rock on which all our theories foundered, that and the message the governess had sent to Charlie Ellingham not to come to the Wells house that night. By no stretch of rather excited imaginations could we imagine Ellingham writing such a letter. Who had written the letter, then, and for whom was it meant?

As to the telephone message, it seemed to preclude the possibility of Ellingham's having gone to the house that night. But the fact remained that a man, as yet unidentified, was undoubtedly concerned in the case, had written the letter, and had probably been in the Wells house the night I went there alone.

In the end, we decided to hold one more seance, and then, unless the further developments were such that we must go on, to let the affair drop.

It is typical of the strained nervous tension which had developed in all of us during the past twelve days, that that night when, having forgotten to let the dog in, my wife and I were roused from a sound sleep by his howling, she would not allow me to go down and admit him.

VIII

On Sunday I went to church. I felt, after the strange phenomena in Mrs. Dane's drawing-room, and after the contact with tragedy to which they had led, that I must hold with a sort of desperation to the traditions and beliefs by which I had hitherto regulated my conduct. And the church did me good. Between the immortality it taught and the theory of spiritualism as we had seen it in action there was a great gulf, and I concluded that this gulf was the soul. The conclusion that mind and certain properties of mind survived was not enough. The thought of a disembodied intelligence was pathetic, depressing. But the thought of a glorified soul was the hope of the world.

My wife, too, was in a penitent and rather exalted mood. During the sermon she sat with her hand in mine, and I was conscious of peace and a deep thankfulness. We had been married for many years, and we had grown very close. Of what importance was the Wells case, or what mattered it that there were strange new-old laws in the universe, so long as we kept together?

That my wife had felt a certain bitterness toward Miss Jeremy, a jealousy of her powers, even of her youth, had not dawned on me. But when, in her new humility, she suggested that we call on the medium that afternoon. I realized that, in her own way, she was making a sort of atonement.

Miss Jeremy lived with an elderly spinster cousin, a short distance out of town. It was a grim house, coldly and rigidly Calvinistic. It gave an unpleasant impression at the start, and our comfort was not increased by the discovery, made early in the call, that the cousin regarded the Neighborhood Club and its members with suspicion.

The cousin—her name was Connell—was small and sharp, and she entered the room followed by a train of cats. All the time she was frigidly greeting us, cats were coming in at the door, one after the other. It fascinated me. I do not like cats. I am, as a matter of confession, afraid of cats. They affect me as do snakes. They trailed in in a seemingly endless procession, and one of them took a fancy to me, and leaped from behind on to my shoulder. The shock set me stammering.

"My cousin is out," said Miss Connell. "Doctor Sperry has taken her for a ride. She will be back very soon."

I shook a cat from my trouser leg, and my wife made an unimportant remark.

"I may as well tell you, I disapprove of what Alice is doing," said Miss Connell. "She doesn't have to. I've offered her a good home. She was brought up a Presbyterian. I call this sort of thing playing with the powers of darkness. Only the eternally damned are doomed to walk the earth. The blessed are at rest."

"But you believe in her powers, don't you?" my wife asked.

"I believe she can do extraordinary things. She saw my father's spirit in this very room last night, and described him, although she had never seen him."

As she had said that only the eternally damned were doomed to walk the earth, I was tempted to comment on this stricture on her departed parent, but a large cat, much scarred with fighting and named Violet, insisted at that moment on crawling into my lap, and my attention was distracted.

"But the whole thing is un-Christian and undignified," Miss Connell proceeded, in her cold voice. "Come, Violet, don't annoy the gentleman. I have other visions of the next life than of rapping on tables and chairs, and throwing small articles about."

It was an extraordinary visit. Even the arrival of Miss Jeremy herself, flushed with the air and looking singularly normal, was hardly a relief. Sperry, who followed, was clearly pleased to see us, however.

It was not hard to see how things were with him. He helped the girl out of her wraps with a manner that was almost proprietary, and drew a chair for her close to the small fire which hardly affected the chill of the room.

With their entrance a spark of hospitality seemed to kindle in the cat lady's breast. It was evident that she liked Sperry. Perhaps she saw in him a method of weaning her cousin from traffic with the powers of darkness. She said something about tea, and went out.

Sperry looked across at the girl and smiled.

"Shall I tell them?" he said.

"I want very much to have them know."

He stood up, and with that unconscious drama which actuates a man at a crisis in his affairs, he put a hand on her shoulder. "This young lady is going to marry me," he said. "We are very happy today."

But I thought he eyed us anxiously. We were very close friends, and he wanted our approval. I am not sure if we were wise. I do not yet know. But something of the new understanding between my wife and myself must have found its way to our voices, for he was evidently satisfied.

"Then that's all right," he said heartily. And my wife, to my surprise, kissed the girl.

Except for the cats, sitting around, the whole thing was strangely normal. And yet, even there, something happened that set me to thinking afterward. Not that it was strange in itself, but that it seemed never possible to get very far away from the Wells mystery.

Tea was brought in by Hawkins!

I knew him immediately, but he did not at once see me. He was evidently accustomed to seeing Sperry there, and he did not recognize my wife. But when he had put down the tray and turned to pick up Sperry's overcoat to carry it into the hall, he saw me. The man actually started. I cannot say that he changed color. He was always a pale, anemic-looking individual. But it was a perceptible instant before he stooped and gathered up the coat.

Sperry turned to me when he had gone out. "That was Hawkins, Horace," he said. "You remember, don't you? The Wellses' butler."

"I knew him at once."

"He wrote to me asking for a position, and I got him this. Looks sick, poor devil. I intend to have a go at his chest."

"How long has he been here?"

"More than a week, I think."

As I drank my tea, I pondered. After all, the Neighborhood Club must guard against the possibility of fraud, and I felt that

Sperry had been indiscreet, to say the least. From the time of Hawkins' service in Miss Jeremy's home there would always be the suspicion of collusion between them. I did not believe it was so, but Herbert, for instance, would be inclined to suspect her. Suppose that Hawkins knew about the crime? Or knew something and surmised the rest?

When we rose to go Sperry drew me aside.

"You think I've made a mistake?"

"I do."

He flung away with an impatient gesture, then came back to me.

"Now look here," he said, "I know what you mean, and the whole idea is absurd. Of course I never thought about it, but even allowing for connivance—which I don't for a moment—the fellow was not in the house at the time of the murder."

"I know he says he was not."

"Even then," he said, "how about the first sitting? I'll swear she had never even heard of him then."

"The fact remains that his presence here makes us all absurd."

"Do you want me to throw him out?"

"I don't see what possible good that will do now."

I was uneasy all the way home. The element of doubt, always so imminent in our dealings with psychic phenomena, had me by the throat. How much did Hawkins know? Was there any way, without going to the police, to find if he had really been out of the Wellses' house that night, now almost two weeks ago, when Arthur Wells had been killed?

That evening I went to Sperry's house, after telephoning that I was coming. On the way I stopped in at Mrs. Dane's and secured something from her. She was wildly curious, and made me promise to go in on my way back, and explain. I made a compromise.

"I will come in if I have anything to tell you," I said.

But I knew, by her grim smile, that she would station herself by her window, and that I would stop, unless I made a detour of three blocks to avoid her. She is a very determined woman.

Sperry was waiting for me in his library, a pleasant room which I have often envied him. Even the most happily married man wishes, now and then, for some quiet, dull room which is essentially his own. My own library is really the family sitting-room, and a Christmas or so ago my wife presented me with a very handsome phonograph instrument. My reading, therefore, is done to music, and the necessity for putting my book down to change the record at times interferes somewhat with my train of thought.

So I entered Sperry's library with appreciation. He was standing by the fire, with the grave face and slightly bent head of his professional manner. We say, in the neighborhood, that Sperry uses his professional manner as armor, so I was rather prepared to do battle; but he forestalled me.

"Horace," he said, "I have been a fool, a driveling idiot. We were getting something at those sittings. Something real. She's wonderful. She's going to give it up, but the fact remains that she has some power we haven't, and now I've discredited her! I see it plainly enough." He was rather bitter about it, but not hostile. His fury was at himself. "Of course," he went on, "I am sure that she got nothing from Hawkins. But the fact remains—" He was hurt in his pride of her.

"I wonder," I said, "if you kept the letter Hawkins wrote you when he asked for a position."

He was not sure. He went into his consulting room and was gone for some time. I took the opportunity to glance over his books and over the room.

Arthur Wells's stick was standing in a corner, and I took it up and examined it. It was an English malacca, light and strong, and had seen service. It was long, too long for me; it occurred to me that Wells had been about my height, and that it was odd that he should have carried so long a stick. There was no ease in swinging it.

From that to the memory of Hawkins's face when Sperry took it, the night of the murder, in the hall of the Wells house, was only a step. I seemed that day to be thinking considerably about Hawkins.

When Sperry returned I laid the stick on the table. There can be no doubt that I did so, for I had to move a book-rack to place it. One end, the handle, was near the ink-well, and the ferrule lay on a copy of Gibson's "Life Beyond the Grave," which Sperry had evidently been reading.

Sperry had found the letter. As I glanced at it I recognized the writing at once, thin and rather sexless, Spencerian.

Dear Sir: Since Mr. Wells's death I am out of employment. Before I took the position of butler with Mr. Wells I was valet to Mr. Ellingham, and before that, in England, to Lord Condray. I have a very good letter of recommendation from Lord Condray. If you need a servant at this time I would do my best to give satisfaction.

Signed ARTHUR HAWKINS.

I put down the application, and took the anonymous letter about the bag from my pocketbook. "Read this, Sperry," I said. "You know the letter. Mrs. Dane read it to us Saturday night. But compare the writing."

He compared the two, with a slight lifting of his eyebrows. Then he put them down. "Hawkins!" he said. "Hawkins has the letters! And the bag!"

"Exactly," I commented dryly. "In other words, Hawkins was in Miss Jeremy's house when, at the second sitting, she told of the letters."

I felt rather sorry for Sperry. He paced the room wretchedly, the two letters in his hand.

"But why should he tell her, if he did?" he demanded. "The writer of that anonymous letter was writing for only one person. Every effort is made to conceal his identity."

I felt that he was right. The point was well taken.

"The question now is, to whom was it written?" We pondered that, to no effect. That Hawkins had certain letters which touched on the Wells affair, that they were probably in his possession in the Connell house, was clear enough. But we had no possible authority for trying to get the letters, although Sperry was anxious to make the attempt.

"Although I feel," he said, "that it is too late to help her very much. She is innocent; I know that. I think you know that, too, deep in that legal mind of yours. It is wrong to discredit her because I did a foolish thing." He warmed to his argument. "Why, think, man," he said. "The whole first sitting was practically coincident with the crime itself."

It was true enough. Whatever suspicion might be cast on the second seance, the first at least remained inexplicable, by any laws we recognized. In a way, I felt sorry for Sperry. Here he was, on the first day of his engagement, protesting her honesty, her complete ignorance of the revelations she had made and his intention to keep her in ignorance, and yet betraying his own anxiety and possible doubt in the same breath.

"She did not even know there was a family named Wells. When I said that Hawkins had been employed by the Wells, it meant nothing to her. I was watching."

So even Sperry was watching. He was in love with her, but his scientific mind, like my legal one, was slow to accept what during the past two weeks it had been asked to accept.

I left him at ten o'clock. Mrs. Dane was still at her window, and her far-sighted old eyes caught me as I tried to steal past. She rapped on the window, and I was obliged to go in. Obliged, too, to tell her of the discovery and, at last, of Hawkins being in the Connell house.

"I want those letters, Horace," she said at last.

"So do I. I'm not going to steal them."

"The question is, where has he got them?"

"The question is, dear lady, that they are not ours to take."

"They are not his, either."

Well, that was true enough. But I had done all the private investigating I cared to. And I told her so. She only smiled cryptically.

So far as I know, Mrs. Dane was the only one among us who had entirely escaped certain strange phenomena during that period, and as I have only so far recorded my own experiences, I shall here place in order the various manifestations made to the other members of the Neighborhood Club during that trying period and in their own words. As none of them have suffered since, a certain allowance must be made for our nervous strain. As before, I shall offer no explanation.

Alice Robinson: On night following second seance saw a light in room, not referable to any outside influence. Was an amorphous body which glowed pallidly and moved about wall over fireplace, gradually coming to stop in a corner, where it faded and disappeared.

Clara, Mrs. Dane's secretary: Had not slept much since first seance. Was frequently conscious that she was not alone in room, but on turning on light room was always empty. Wakened twice with sense of extreme cold. I have recorded my own similar experience.

Sperry has consistently maintained that he had no experiences whatever during that period, but admits that he heard various knockings in his bedroom at night, which he attributed to the lighting of his furnace, and the resulting expansion of the furniture due to heat.

Herbert Robinson: Herbert was the most difficult member of the Club from whom to secure data, but he has recently confessed that he was wakened one night by the light falling on to his bed from a picture which hung on the wall over his mantelpiece, and which stood behind a clock, two glass vases and a pair of candlesticks. The door of his room was locked at the time.

Mrs. Johnson: Had a great many minor disturbances, so that on rousing one night to find me closing a window against a storm she thought I was a spectre, and to this day insists that I only entered her room when I heard her scream. For this reason I have made no record of her various experiences, as I felt that her nervous condition precluded accurate observation.

As in all records of psychic phenomena, the human element must be considered, and I do not attempt either to analyze these various phenomena or to explain them. Herbert, for instance, has been known to walk in his sleep. But I respectfully offer, as opposed to this, that my watch has never been known to walk at all, and that Mrs. Johnson's bracelet could hardly be accused of an attack of nerves.

IX

The following day was Monday. When I came downstairs I found a neat bundle lying in the hall, and addressed to me. My wife had followed me down, and we surveyed it together.

I had a curious feeling about the parcel, and was for cutting the cord with my knife. But my wife is careful about string. She has always fancied that the time would come when we would need some badly, and it would not be around. I have an entire drawer of my chiffonier, which I really need for other uses, filled with bundles of twine, pink, white and brown. I recall, on one occasion, packing a suit-case in the dusk, in great hasty, and emptying the drawer containing my undergarments into it, to discover, when I opened it on the train for my pajamas, nothing but rolls of cord and several packages of Christmas ribbons. So I was obliged to wait until she had untied the knots by means of a hairpin.

It was my overcoat! My overcoat, apparently uninjured, but with the collection of keys I had made missing.

The address was printed, not written, in a large, strong hand, with a stub pen. I did not, at the time, notice the loss of certain papers which had been in the breast pocket. I am rather absent-minded, and it was not until the night after the third sitting that they were recalled to my mind.

At something after eleven Herbert Robinson called me up at my office. He was at Sperry's house, Sperry having been his physician during his recent illness.

"I say, Horace, this is Herbert."

"Yes. How are you?"

"Doing well, Sperry says. I'm at his place now. I'm speaking for him. He's got a patient."

"Yes."

"You were here last night, he says." Herbert has a circumlocutory manner over the phone which irritates me. He begins slowly and does not know how to stop. Talk with him drags on endlessly.

"Well, I admit it," I snapped. "It's not a secret."

He lowered his voice. "Do you happen to have noticed a walking-stick in the library when you were here?"

"Which walking-stick?"

"You know. The one we—"

"Yes. I saw it."

"You didn't, by any chance, take it home with you?"

"No."

"Are you sure?"

"Certainly I'm sure."

"You are an absent-minded beggar, you know," he explained. "You remember about the fire-tongs. And a stick is like an umbrella. One is likely to pick it up and—"

"One is not likely to do anything of the sort. At least, I didn't."

"Oh, all right. Every one well?"

"Very well, thanks."

"Suppose we'll see you tonight?"

"Not unless you ring off and let me do some work," I said irritably.

He rang off. I was ruffled, I admit; but I was uneasy, also. To tell the truth, the affair of the fire-tongs had cost me my self-confidence. I called up my wife, and she said Herbert was a fool and Sperry also. But she made an exhaustive search of the premises, without result. Whoever had taken the stick, I was cleared. Cleared, at least, for a time. There were strange developments coming that threatened my peace of mind.

It was that day that I discovered that I was being watched. Shadowed, I believe is the technical word. I daresay I had been followed from my house, but I had not noticed. When I went out to lunch a youngish man in a dark overcoat was waiting for the elevator, and I saw him again when I came out of my house. We went downtown again on the same car.

Perhaps I would have thought nothing of it, had I not been summoned to the suburbs on a piece of business concerning a mortgage. He was at the far end of the platform as I took the train to return to the city, with his back to me. I lost him in the crowd at the downtown station, but he evidently had not lost me, for, stopping to buy a newspaper, I turned, and, as my pause had evidently been unexpected, he almost ran into me.

With that tendency of any man who finds himself under suspicion to search his past for some dereliction, possibly forgotten, I puzzled over the situation for some time that afternoon. I did not connect it with the Wells case, for in that matter I was indisputably the hunter, not the hunted.

Although I found no explanation for the matter, I did not tell my wife that evening. Women are strange and she would, I feared, immediately jump to the conclusion that there was something in my private life that I was keeping from her.

Almost all women, I have found, although not over-conscious themselves of the charm and attraction of their husbands, are of the conviction that these husbands exert a dangerous fascination over other women, and that this charm, which does not reveal itself in the home circle, is used abroad with occasionally disastrous effect.

My preoccupation, however, did not escape my wife, and she commented on it at dinner.

"You are generally dull, Horace," she said, "but tonight you are deadly."

After dinner I went into our reception room, which is not lighted unless we are expecting guests, and peered out of the window. The detective, or whoever he might be, was walking negligently up the street.

As that was the night of the third seance, I find that my record covers the fact that Mrs. Dane was housecleaning, for which reason we had not been asked to dinner, that my wife and I dined early, at six-thirty, and that it was seven o'clock when Sperry called me by telephone.

"Can you come to my office at once?" he asked. "I dare say Mrs. Johnson won't mind going to the Dane house alone."

"Is there anything new?"

"No. But I want to get into the Wells house again. Bring the keys."

"They were in the overcoat. It came back today, but the keys are missing."

"Did you lock the back door?"

"I don't remember. No, of course not. I didn't have the keys."

"Then there's a chance," he observed, after a moment's pause. "Anyhow, it's worth trying. Herbert told you about the stick?"

"Yes. I never had it, Sperry."

Fortunately, during this conversation my wife was upstairs dressing. I knew quite well that she would violently oppose a second visit on my part to the deserted house down the street. I therefore left a message for her that I had gone on, and, finding the street clear, met Sperry at his door-step.

"This is the last sitting, Horace," he explained, "and I feel we ought to have the most complete possible knowledge, beforehand. We will be in a better position to understand what comes. There are two or three things we haven't checked up on."

He slipped an arm through mine, and we started down the street. "I'm going to get to the bottom of this, Horace, old dear," he said.

"Remember, we're pledged to a psychic investigation only."

"Rats!" he said rudely. "We are going to find out who killed Arthur Wells, and if he deserves hanging we'll hang him."

"Or her?"

"It wasn't Elinor Wells," he said positively. "Here's the point: if he's been afraid to go back for his overcoat it's still there. I don't expect that, however. But the thing about the curtain interests me. I've been reading over my copy of the notes on the sittings. It was said, you remember, that curtains—some curtains—would have been better places to hide the letters than the bag."

I stopped suddenly. "By Jove, Sperry," I said. "I remember now. My notes of the sittings were in my overcoat."

"And they are gone?"

"They are gone."

He whistled softly. "That's unfortunate," he said. "Then the other person, whoever he is, knows what we know!"

He was considerably startled when I told him I had been shadowed, and insisted that it referred directly to the case in hand. "He's got your notes," he said, "and he's got to know what your next move is going to be."

His intention, I found, was to examine the carpet outside of the dressing-room door, and the floor beneath it, to discover if possible whether Arthur Wells had fallen there and been moved.

"Because I think you are right," he said. "He wouldn't have been likely to shoot himself in a hall, and because the very moving of the body would be in itself suspicious. Then I want to look at the curtains. 'The curtains would have been safer.' Safer for what? For the bag with the letters, probably, for she followed that with the talk about Hawkins. He'd got them, and somebody was afraid he had."

"Just where does Hawkins come in, Sperry?" I asked.

"I'm damned if I know," he reflected. "We may learn tonight."

The Wells house was dark and forbidding. We walked past it once, as an officer was making his rounds in leisurely fashion, swinging his night-stick in circles. But on our return the street was empty, and we turned in at the side entry.

I led the way with comparative familiarity. It was, you will remember, my third similar excursion. With Sperry behind me I felt confident.

"In case the door is locked, I have a few skeleton keys," said Sperry.

We had reached the end of the narrow passage, and emerged into the square of brick and grass that lay behind the house. While the night was clear, the place lay in comparative darkness. Sperry stumbled over something, and muttered to himself.

The rear porch lay in deep shadow. We went up the steps together. Then Sperry stopped, and I advanced to the doorway. It was locked.

With my hand on the door-knob, I turned to Sperry. He was struggling violently with a dark figure, and even as I turned they went over with a crash and rolled together down the steps. Only one of them rose.

I was terrified. I confess it. It was impossible to see whether it was Sperry or his assailant. If it was Sperry who lay in a heap on the ground, I felt that I was lost. I could not escape. The way was blocked, and behind me the door, to which I now turned frantically, was a barrier I could not move.

Then, out of the darkness behind me, came Sperry's familiar, booming bass. "I've knocked him out, I'm afraid. Got a match, Horace?"

Much shaken, I went down the steps and gave Sperry a wooden toothpick, under the impression that it was a match. That rectified, we bent over the figure on the bricks.

"Knocked out, for sure," said Sperry, "but I think it's not serious. A watchman, I suppose. Poor devil, we'll have to get him into the house."

The lock gave way to manipulation at last, and the door swung open. There came to us the heavy odor of all closed houses, a combination of carpets, cooked food, and floor wax. My nerves, now taxed to their utmost, fairly shrank from it, but Sperry was cool.

He bore the brunt of the weight as we carried the watchman in, holding him with his arms dangling, helpless and rather pathetic. Sperry glanced around.

"Into the kitchen," he said. "We can lock him in."

We had hardly laid him on the floor when I heard the slow stride of the officer of the beat. He had turned into the paved alley-way, and was advancing with measured, ponderous steps. Fortunately I am an agile man, and thus I was able to get to the outer door, reverse the key and turn it from the inside, before I heard him hailing the watchman.

"Hello there!" he called. "George, I say! George!"

He listened for a moment, then came up and tried the door. I crouched inside, as guilty as the veriest house-breaker in the business. But he had no suspicion, clearly, for he turned and went away, whistling as he went.

Not until we heard him going down the street again, absently running his night-stick along the fence palings, did Sperry or I move.

"A narrow squeak, that," I said, mopping my face.

"A miss is as good as a mile," he observed, and there was a sort of exultation in his voice. He is a born adventurer.

He came out into the passage and quickly locked the door behind him.

"Now, friend Horace," he said, "if you have anything but toothpicks for matches, we will look for the overcoat, and then we will go upstairs."

"Suppose he wakens and raises an alarm?"

"We'll be out of luck. That's all."

As we had anticipated, there was no overcoat in the library, and after listening a moment at the kitchen door, we ascended a rear staircase to the upper floor. I had, it will be remembered, fallen from a chair on a table in the dressing room, and had left them thus overturned when I charged the third floor. The room, however, was now in perfect order, and when I held my candle to the ceiling, I perceived that the bullet hole had again been repaired, and this time with such skill that I could not even locate it.

"We are up against some one cleverer than we are, Sperry," I acknowledged.

"And who has more to lose than we have to gain," he added cheerfully. "Don't worry about that, Horace. You're a married man and I'm not. If a woman wanted to hide some letters from her husband, and chose a curtain for a receptacle, what room would hide them in. Not in his dressing-room, eh?"

He took the candle and led the way to Elinor Wells's bedroom. Here, however, the draperies were down, and we would have been at a loss, had I not remembered my wife's custom of folding draperies when we close the house, and placing them under the dusting sheets which cover the various beds.

Our inspection of the curtains was hurried, and broken by various excursions on my part to listen for the watchman. But he remained quiet below, and finally we found what we were looking for. In the lining of one of the curtains, near the bottom, a long, ragged cut had been made.

"Cut in a hurry, with curved scissors," was Sperry's comment. "Probably manicure scissors."

The result was a sort of pocket in the curtain, concealed on the chintz side, which was the side which would hang toward the room.

"Probably," he said, "the curtain would have been better. It would have stayed anyhow. Whereas the bag—" He was flushed with triumph. "How in the world would Hawkins know that?" he demanded. "You can talk all you like. She's told us things that no one ever told her."

Before examining the floor in the hall I went downstairs and listened outside the kitchen door. The watchman was stirring inside the room, and groaning occasionally. Sperry, however, when I told him, remained cool and in his exultant mood, and I saw that he meant to vindicate Miss Jeremy if he flung me into jail and the newspapers while doing it.

"We'll have a go at the floors under the carpets now," he said. "If he gets noisy, you can go down with the fire-tongs. I understand you are an expert with them."

The dressing-room had a large rug, like the nursery above it, and turning back the carpet was a simple matter. There had been a stain beneath where the dead man's head had lain, but it had been scrubbed and scraped away. The boards were white for an area of a square foot or so.

Sperry eyed the spot with indifference. "Not essential," he said. "Shows good housekeeping. That's all. The point is, are there other spots?"

And, after a time, we found what we were after. The upper hall was carpeted, and my penknife came into requisition to lift the tacks. They came up rather easily, as if but recently put in. That, indeed, proved to be the case.

Just outside the dressing-room door the boards for an area of two square feet or more beneath the carpet had been scraped and scrubbed. With the lifting of the carpet came, too, a strong odor, as of ammonia. But the stain of blood had absolutely disappeared.

Sperry, kneeling on the floor with the candle held close, examined the wood. "Not only scrubbed," he said, "but scraped down, probably with a floor-scraper. It's pretty clear, Horace. The poor devil fell here. There was a struggle, and he went down. He lay there for a while, too, until some plan was thought out. A man does not usually kill himself in a hallway. It's a sort of solitary deed. He fell here, and was dragged into the room. The angle of the bullet in the ceiling would probably show it came from here, too, and went through the doorway."

We were startled at that moment by a loud banging below. Sperry leaped to his feet and caught up his hat.

"The watchman," he said. "We'd better get out. He'll have all the neighbors in at that rate."

He was still hammering on the door as we went down the rear stairs, and Sperry stood outside the door and to one side.

"Keep out of range, Horace," he cautioned me. And to the watchman:

"Now, George, we will put the key under the door, and in ten minutes you may come out. Don't come sooner. I've warned you."

By the faint light from outside I could see him stooping, not in front of the door, but behind it. And it was well he did, for the moment the key was on the other side, a shot zipped through one of the lower panels. I had not expected it and it set me to shivering.

"No more of that, George," said Sperry calmly and cheerfully. "This is a quiet neighborhood, and we don't like shooting. What is more, my friend here is very expert with his own particular weapon, and at any moment he may go to the fire-place in the library and—"

I have no idea why Sperry chose to be facetious at that time, and my resentment rises as I record it. For when we reached the yard we heard the officer running along the alley-way, calling as he ran.

"The fence, quick," Sperry said.

I am not very good at fences, as a rule, but I leaped that one like a cat, and came down in a barrel of waste-paper on the other side. Getting me out was a breathless matter, finally accomplished by turning the barrel over so that I could crawl out. We could hear the excited voices of the two men beyond the fence, and we ran. I was better than Sperry at that. I ran like a rabbit. I never even felt my legs. And Sperry pounded on behind me.

We heard, behind us, one of the men climbing the fence. But in jumping down he seemed to have struck the side of the overturned barrel. Probably it rolled and threw him, for that part of my mind which was not intent on flight heard him fall, and curse loudly.

"Go to it," Sperry panted behind me. "Roll over and break your neck."

This, I need hardly explain, was meant for our pursuer.

We turned a corner and were out on one of the main thoroughfares. Instantly, so innate is cunning to the human brain, we fell to walking sedately.

It was as well that we did, for we had not gone a half block before we saw our policeman again, lumbering toward us and blowing a whistle as he ran.

"Stop and get this street-car," Sperry directed me. "And don't breathe so hard."

The policeman stared at us fixedly, stopping to do so, but all he saw was two well-dressed and professional-looking men, one of them rather elderly who was hailing a street-car. I had the presence of mind to draw my watch and consult it.

"Just in good time," I said distinctly, and we mounted the car step. Sperry remained on the platform and lighted a cigar. This gave him a chance to look back.

"Rather narrow squeak, that," he observed, as he came in and sat down beside me. "Your gray hairs probably saved us."

I was quite numb from the waist down, from my tumble and from running, and it was some time before I could breathe quietly. Suddenly Sperry fell to laughing.

"I wish you could have seen yourself in that barrel, and crawling out," he said.

We reached Mrs. Dane's, to find that Miss Jeremy had already arrived, looking rather pale, as I had noticed she always did before a seance. Her color had faded, and her eyes seemed sunken in her head.

"Not ill, are you?" Sperry asked her, as he took her hand.

"Not at all. But I am anxious. I always am. These things do not come for the calling."

"This is the last time. You have promised."

"Yes. The last time."

X

It appeared that Herbert Robinson had been reading, during his convalescence, a considerable amount of psychic literature, and that we were to hold this third and final sitting under test conditions. As before, the room had been stripped of furniture, and the cloth and rod which formed the low screen behind Miss Jeremy's chair were not of her own providing, but Herbert's.

He had also provided, for some reason or other, eight small glass cups, into which he placed the legs of the two tables, and in a business-like manner he set out on the large stand a piece of white paper, a pencil, and a spool of black thread. It is characteristic of Miss Jeremy, and of her own ignorance of the methods employed in professional seances, that she was as much interested and puzzled as we were.

When he had completed his preparations, Herbert made a brief speech.

"Members of the Neighborhood Club," he said impressively, "we have agreed among ourselves that this is to be our last meeting for the purpose that is before us. I have felt, therefore, that in justice to the medium this final seance should leave us with every conviction of its genuineness. Whatever phenomena occur, the medium must be, as she has been, above suspicion. For the replies of her 'control,' no particular precaution seems necessary, or possible. But the first seance divided itself into two parts: an early period when, so far as we could observe, the medium was at least partly conscious, possibly fully so, when physical demonstrations occurred. And a second, or trance period, during which we received replies to questions. It is for the physical phenomena that I am about to take certain precautions."

"Are you going to tie me?" Miss Jeremy asked.

"Do you object?"

"Not at all. But with what?"

"With silk thread," Herbert said, smilingly.

She held out her wrists at once, but Herbert placed her in her chair, and proceeded to wrap her, chair and all, in a strong network of fine threads, drawn sufficiently taut to snap with any movement.

He finished by placing her feet on the sheet of paper, and outlining their position there with a pencil line.

The proceedings were saved from absurdity by what we all felt was the extreme gravity of the situation. There were present in the room Mrs. Dane, the Robinsons, Sperry, my wife and myself. Clara, Mrs. Dane's secretary, had begged off on the plea of nervousness from the earlier and physical portion of the seance, and was to remain outside in the hall until the trance commenced.

Sperry objected to this, as movement in the circle during the trance had, in the first seance, induced fretful uneasiness in the medium. But Clara, appealed to, begged to be allowed to remain outside until she was required, and showed such unmistakable nervousness that we finally agreed.

"Would a slight noise disturb her?" Mrs. Dane asked.

Miss Jeremy thought not, if the circle remained unbroken, and Mrs. Dane considered.

"Bring me my stick from the hall, Horace," she said. "And tell Clara I'll rap on the floor with it when I want her."

I found a stick in the rack outside and brought it in. The lights were still on in the chandelier overhead, and as I gave the stick to Mrs. Dane I heard Sperry speaking sharply behind me.

"Where did you get that stick?" he demanded.

"In the hall. I—"

"I never saw it before," said Mrs. Dane. "Perhaps it is Herbert's."

But I caught Sperry's eye. We had both recognized it. It was Arthur Wells's, the one which Sperry had taken from his room, and which, in turn, had been taken from Sperry's library.

Sperry was watching me with a sort of cynical amusement.

"You're an absent-minded beggar, Horace," he said.

"You didn't, by any chance, stop here on your way back from my place the other night, did you?"

"I did. But I didn't bring that thing."

"Look here, Horace," he said, more gently, "you come in and see me some day soon. You're not as fit as you ought to be."

I confess to a sort of helpless indignation that was far from the composure the occasion required. But the others, I believe, were fully convinced that no human agency had operated to bring the stick into Mrs. Dane's house, a belief that prepared them for anything that might occur.

A number of things occurred almost as soon as the lights were out, interrupting a train of thought in which I saw myself in the first stages of mental decay, and carrying about the streets not only fire-tongs and walking-sticks, but other portable property belonging to my friends.

Perhaps my excitement had a bad effect on the medium. She was uneasy and complained that the threads that bound her arms were tight. She was distinctly fretful. But after a time she settled down in her chair. Her figure, a deeper shadow in the semi-darkness of the room, seemed sagged—seemed, in some indefinable way, smaller. But there was none of the stertorous breathing that preceded trance.

Then, suddenly, a bell that Sperry had placed on the stand beyond the black curtain commenced to ring. It rang at first gently, then violently. It made a hideous clamor. I had a curious sense that it was ringing up in the air, near the top of the curtain. It was a relief to have it thrown to the ground, its racket silenced.

Quite without warning, immediately after, my chair twisted under me. "I am being turned around," I said, in a low tone. "It as if something has taken hold of the back of the chair, and is twisting it. It has stopped now." I had been turned fully a quarter round.

For five minutes, by the luminous dial of my watch on the table before me, nothing further occurred, except that the black curtain appeared to swell, as in a wind.

"There is something behind it," Alice Robinson said, in a terrorized tone. "Something behind it, moving."

"It is not possible," Herbert assured her. "Nothing, that is—there is only one door, and it is closed. I have examined the walls and floor carefully."

At the end of five minutes something soft and fragrant fell on to the table near me. I had not noticed Herbert when he placed the flowers from Mrs. Dane's table on the stand, and I was more startled than the others. Then the glass prisms in the chandelier over our heads clinked together, as if they had been swept by a finger. More of the flowers came. We were pelted with them. And into the quiet that followed there came a light, fine but steady tattoo on the table in our midst. Then at last silence, and the medium in deep trance, and Mrs. Dane rapping on the floor for Clara.

When Clara came in, Mrs. Dane told her to switch on the lights. Miss Jeremy had dropped in her chair until the silk across her chest was held taut. But investigation showed that none of the threads were broken and that her evening slippers still fitted into the outline on the paper beneath them. Without getting up, Sperry reached to the stand behind Miss Jeremy, and brought into view a piece of sculptor's clay he had placed there. The handle of the bell was now jammed into the mass. He had only time to show it to us when the medium began to speak.

I find, on re-reading the earlier part of this record, that I have omitted mention of Miss Jeremy's "control." So suddenly had we jumped, that first evening, into the trail that led us to the Wells case, that beyond the rather raucous "good-evening," and possibly the extraneous matter referring to Mother Goose and so on, we had been saved the usual preliminary patter of the average control.

On this night, however, we were obliged to sit impatiently through a rambling discourse, given in a half-belligerent manner, on the deterioration of moral standards. Re-reading Clara's notes, I find that the subject matter is without originality and the diction inferior. But the lecture ceased abruptly, and the time for questions had come.

"Now," Herbert said, "we want you to go back to the house where you saw the dead man on the floor. You know his name, don't you?"

There was a pause. "Yes. Of course I do. A. L. Wells."

Arthur had been known to most of us by his Christian name, but the initials were correct.

"How do you know it is an L.?"

"On letters," was the laconic answer. Then: "Letters, letters, who has the letters?"

"Do you know whose cane this is?"

"Yes."

"Will you tell us?"

Up to that time the replies had come easily and quickly. But beginning with the cane question, the medium was in difficulties. She moved uneasily, and spoke irritably. The replies were slow and grudging. Foreign subjects were introduced, as now.

"Horace's wife certainly bullies him," said the voice. "He's afraid of her. And the fire-tongs—the fire-tongs—the fire-tongs!"

"Whose cane is this?" Herbert repeated.

"Mr. Ellingham's."

This created a profound sensation.

"How do you know that?"

"He carried it at the seashore. He wrote in the sand with it."

"What did he write?"

"Ten o'clock."

"He wrote 'ten o'clock' in the sand, and the waves came and washed it away?"

"Yes."

"Horace," said my wife, leaning forward, "why not ask her about that stock of mine? If it is going down, I ought to sell, oughtn't I?"

Herbert eyed her with some exasperation.

"We are here to make a serious investigation," he said. "If the members of the club will keep their attention on what we are doing, we may get somewhere. Now," to the medium, "the man is dead, and the revolver is beside him. Did he kill himself?"

"No. He attacked her when he found the letters."

"And she shot him?"

"I can't tell you that."

"Try very hard. It is important."

"I don't know," was the fretful reply. "She may have. She hated him. I don't know. She says she did."

"She says she killed him?"

But there was no reply to this, although Herbert repeated it several times.

Instead, the voice of the "control" began to recite a verse of poetry—a cheap, sentimental bit of trash. It was maddening, under the circumstances.

"Do you know where the letters are?"

"Hawkins has them."

"They were not hidden in the curtain?" This was Sperry.

"No. The police might have searched the room."

"Where were these letters?"

There was no direct reply to this, but instead:

"He found them when he was looking for his razorstrop. They were in the top of a closet. His revolver was there, too. He went back and got it. It was terrible."

There was a profound silence, followed by a slight exclamation from Sperry as he leaped to his feet. The screen at the end of the room, which cut off the light from Clara's candle, was toppling. The next instant it fell, and we saw Clara sprawled over her table, in a dead faint.

XI

In this, the final chapter of the record of these seances, I shall give, as briefly as possible, the events of the day following the third sitting. I shall explain the mystery of Arthur Wells's death, and I shall give the solution arrived at by the Neighborhood Club as to the strange communications from the medium, Miss Jeremy, now Sperry's wife.

But there are some things I cannot explain. Do our spirits live on, on this earth plane, now and then obedient to the wills of those yet living? Is death, then, only a gateway into higher space, from which, through the open door of a "sensitive" mind, we may be brought back on occasion to commit the inadequate absurdities of the physical seance?

Or is Sperry right, and do certain individuals manifest powers of a purely physical nature, but powers which Sperry characterizes as the survival of some long-lost development by which at one time we knew how to liberate a forgotten form of energy?

Who can say? We do not know. We have had to accept these things as they have been accepted through the ages, and give them either a spiritual or a purely natural explanation, as our minds happen to be adventurous or analytic in type.

But outside of the purely physical phenomena of those seances, we are provided with an explanation which satisfies the Neighborhood Club, even if it fails to satisfy the convinced spiritist. We have been accused merely of substituting one mystery for another, but I reply by saying that the mystery we substitute is not a mystery, but an acknowledged fact.

On Tuesday morning I wakened after an uneasy night. I knew certain things, knew them definitely in the clear light of morning. Hawkins had the letters that Arthur Wells had found; that was one thing. I had not taken Ellingham's stick to Mrs. Dane's house; that was another. I had not done it. I had placed it on the table and had not touched it again.

But those were immaterial, compared with one outstanding fact. Any supernatural solution would imply full knowledge by whatever power had controlled the medium. And there was not full knowledge. There was, on the contrary, a definite place beyond which the medium could not go.

She did not know who had killed Arthur Wells.

To my surprise, Sperry and Herbert Robinson came together to see me that morning at my office. Sperry, like myself, was pale and tired, but Herbert was restless and talkative, for all the world like a terrier on the scent of a rat.

They had brought a newspaper account of an attempt by burglars to rob the Wells house, and the usual police formula that arrests were expected to be made that day. There was a diagram of the house, and a picture of the kitchen door, with an arrow indicating the bullet-hole.

"Hawkins will be here soon," Sperry said, rather casually, after I had read the clipping.

"Here?"

"Yes. He is bringing a letter from Miss Jeremy. The letter is merely a blind. We want to see him."

Herbert was examining the door of my office. He set the spring lock. "He may try to bolt," he explained. "We're in this pretty deep, you know."

"How about a record of what he says?" Sperry asked.

I pressed a button, and Miss Joyce came in. "Take the testimony of the man who is coming in, Miss Joyce," I directed. "Take everything we say, any of us. Can you tell the different voices?"

She thought she could, and took up her position in the next room, with the door partly open.

I can still see Hawkins as Sperry let him in—a tall, cadaverous man of good manners and an English accent, a superior servant. He was cool but rather resentful. I judged that he considered carrying letters as in no way a part of his work, and that he was careful of his dignity. "Miss Jeremy sent this, sir," he said.

Then his eyes took in Sperry and Herbert, and he drew himself up.

"I see," he said. "It wasn't the letter, then?"

"Not entirely. We want to have a talk with you, Hawkins."

"Very well, sir." But his eyes went from one to the other of us.

"You were in the employ of Mr. Wells. We know that. Also we saw you there the night he died, but some time after his death. What time did you get in that night?"

"About midnight. I am not certain."

"Who told you of what had happened?"

"I told you that before. I met the detectives going out."

"Exactly. Now, Hawkins, you had come in, locked the door, and placed the key outside for the other servants?"

"Yes, sir."

"How do you expect us to believe that?" Sperry demanded irritably. "There was only one key. Could you lock yourself in and then place the key outside?"

"Yes, sir," he replied impassively. "By opening the kitchen window, I could reach out and hang it on the nail."

"You were out of the house, then, at the time Mr. Wells died?"

"I can prove it by as many witnesses as you wish to call."

"Now, about these letters, Hawkins," Sperry said. "The letters in the bag. Have you still got them?"

He half rose—we had given him a chair facing the light—and then sat down again. "What letters?"

"Don't beat about the bush. We know you have the letters. And we want them."

"I don't intend to give them up, sir."

"Will you tell us how you got them?" He hesitated. "If you do not know already, I do not care to say."

I placed the letter to A 31 before him. "You wrote this, I think?" I said.

He was genuinely startled. More than that, indeed, for his face twitched. "Suppose I did?" he said, "I'm not admitting it."

"Will you tell us for whom it was meant?"

"You know a great deal already, gentlemen. Why not find that out from where you learned the rest?"

"You know, then, where we learned what we know?"

"Mrs. Wells suggested that we come here, Horace," he began. "We may need a legal mind on this. I'm not sure, or rather I think it unlikely. But just in case—suppose you tell him, Elinor."

I have no record of the story Elinor Wells told that night in our little reception-room, with Clara sitting in a corner, grave and white. It was fragmentary, inco-ordinate. But I got it all at last.

Charlie Ellingham had killed Arthur Wells, but in a struggle. In parts the story was sordid enough. She did not spare herself, or her motives. She had wanted luxury, and Arthur had not succeeded as he had promised. They were in debt, and living beyond their means. But even that, she hastened to add, would not have mattered, had he not been brutal with her. He had made her life very wretched.

But on the subject of Charlie Ellingham she was emphatic. She knew that there had been talk, but there had been no real basis for it. She had turned to him for comfort, and he gave her love. She didn't know where he was now, and didn't greatly care, but she would like to recover and destroy some letters he had written her.

She was looking crushed and ill, and she told her story incoordinately and nervously. Reduced to its elements, it was as follows:

On the night of Arthur Wells's death they were dressing for a ball. She had made a private arrangement with Ellingham to plead a headache at the last moment and let Arthur go alone. But he had been so insistent that she had been forced to go, after all. She had sent the governess, Suzanne Gautier, out to telephone Ellingham not to come, but he was not at his house, and the message was left with his valet. As it turned out, he had already started.

Elinor was dressed, all but her ball-gown, and had put on a negligee, to wait for the governess to return and help her. Arthur was in his dressing-room, and she heard him grumbling about having no blades for his safety razor.

He got out a case of razors and searched for the strop. When she remembered where the strop was, it was too late. The letters had been beside it, and he was coming toward her, with them in his hand.

She was terrified. He had read only one, but that was enough. He muttered something and turned away. She saw his face as he went toward where the revolver had been hidden from the children, and she screamed.

Charlie Ellingham heard her. The door had been left unlocked by the governess, and he was in the lower hall. He ran up and the two men grappled. The first shot was fired by Arthur. It struck the ceiling. The second she was doubtful about. She thought the revolver was still in Arthur's hand. It was all horrible. He went down like a stone, in the hallway outside the door.

They were nearly mad, the two of them. They had dragged the body in, and then faced each other. Ellingham was for calling the police at once and surrendering, but she had kept him away from the telephone. She maintained, and I think it very possible, that her whole thought was for the children, and the effect on their after lives of such a scandal. And, after all, nothing could help the man on the floor.

It was while they were trying to formulate some concerted plan that they heard footsteps below, and, thinking it was Mademoiselle Gautier, she drove Ellingham into the rear of the house, from which later he managed to escape. But it was Clara who was coming up the stairs.

"She had been our first governess for the children," Elinor said, "and she often came in. She had made a birthday smock for Buddy, and she had it in her hand. She almost fainted. I couldn't tell her about Charlie Ellingham. I couldn't. I told her we had been struggling, and that I was afraid I had shot him. She is quick. She knew just what to do. We worked fast. She said a suicide would not have fired one shot into the ceiling, and she fixed that. It was terrible. And all the time he lay there, with his eyes half open—"

The letters, it seems, were all over the place. Elinor thought of the curtain, cut a receptacle for them, but she was afraid of the police. Finally she gave them to Clara, who was to take them away and burn them.

They did everything they could think of, all the time listening for Suzanne Gautier's return; filled the second empty chamber of the revolver, dragged the body out of the hall and washed the carpet, and called Doctor Sperry, knowing that he was at Mrs. Dane's and could not come.

Clara had only a little time, and with the letters in her handbag she started down the stairs. There she heard some one, possibly Ellingham, on the back stairs, and in her haste, she fell, hurting her knee, and she must have dropped the handbag at that time. They knew now that Hawkins had found it later on. But for a few days they didn't know, and hence the advertisement.

"I think we would better explain Hawkins," Sperry said. "Hawkins was married to Miss Clara here, some years ago, while she was with Mrs. Wells. They had kept it a secret, and recently she has broken with him."

"He was infatuated with another woman," Clara said briefly. "That's a personal matter. It has nothing to do with this case."

"It explains Hawkins's letter."

"It doesn't explain how that medium knew everything that happened," Clara put in, excitedly. "She knew it all, even the library paste! I can tell you, Mr. Johnson, I was close to fainting a dozen times before I finally did it."

"Did you know of our seances?" I asked Mrs. Wells.

"Yes. I may as well tell you that I haven't been in Florida. How could I? The children are there, but I—"

"Did you tell Charlie Ellingham about them?"

"After the second one I warned him, and I think he went to the house. One bullet was somewhere in the ceiling, or in the floor of the nursery. I thought it ought to be found. I don't know whether he found it or not. I've been afraid to see him."

She sat, clasping and unclasping her hands in her lap. She was a proud woman, and surrender had come hard. The struggle was marked in her face. She looked as though she had not slept for days.

"You think I am frightened," she said slowly. "And I am, terribly frightened. But not about discovery. That has come, and cannot be helped."

"Then why?"

"How does this woman, this medium, know these things?" Her voice rose, with an unexpected hysterical catch. "It is superhuman. I am almost mad."

"We're going to get to the bottom of this," Sperry said soothingly. "Be sure that it is not what you think it is, Elinor. There's a simple explanation, and I think I've got it. What about the stick that was taken from my library?"

"Will you tell me how you came to have it, doctor?"

"Yes. I took it from the lower hall the night—the night it happened."

"It was Charlie Ellingham's. He had left it there. We had to have it, doctor. Alone it might not mean much, but with the other things you knew—tell them, Clara."

"I stole it from your office," Clara said, looking straight ahead. "We had to have it. I knew at the second sitting that it was his."

"When did you take it?"

"On Monday morning, I went for Mrs. Dane's medicine, and you had promised her a book. Do you remember? I told your man, and he allowed me to go up to the library. It was there, on the table. I had expected to have to search for it, but it was lying out. I fastened it to my belt, under my long coat."

"And placed it in the rack at Mrs. Dane's?" Sperry was watching her intently, with the same sort of grim intentness he wears when examining a chest.

"I put it in the closet in my room. I meant to get rid of it, when I had a little time. I don't know how it got downstairs, but I think—"

"Yes?"

"We are house-cleaning. A housemaid was washing closets. I suppose she found it and, thinking it was one of Mrs. Dane's, took it downstairs. That is, unless—" It was clear that, like Elinor, she had a supernatural explanation in her mind. She looked gaunt and haggard.

"Mr. Ellingham was anxious to get it," she finished. "He had taken Mr. Johnson's overcoat by mistake one night when you were both in the house, and the notes were in it. He saw that the stick was important."

"Clara," Sperry asked, "did you see, the day you advertised for your bag, another similar advertisement?"

"I saw it. It frightened me."

"You have no idea who inserted it?"

"None whatever."

****

As I have said, the Neighborhood Club ended its investigations with this conclusion, which I believe is properly reached. It is only fair to state that there are those among us who have accepted that theory in the Wells case, but who have preferred to consider that behind both it and the physical phenomena of the seances there was an intelligence which directed both, an intelligence not of this world as we know it. Both Herbert and Alice Robinson are now pronounced spiritualists, although Miss Jeremy, now Mrs. Sperry, has definitely abandoned all investigative work.

Personally, I have evolved no theory. It seems beyond dispute that certain individuals can read minds, and that these same, or other so-called "sensitives," are capable of liberating a form of invisible energy which, however, they turn to no further account than the useless ringing of bells, moving of small tables, and flinging about of divers objects.

To me, I admit, the solution of the Wells case as one of mind-reading is more satisfactory than explanatory. For mental waves remain a mystery, acknowledged, as is electricity, but of a nature yet unrevealed. Thoughts are things. That is all we know.

Mrs. Dane, I believe, had suspected the solution from the start.

The Neighborhood Club has recently disbanded. We tried other things, but we had been spoiled. Our Kipling winter was a failure. We read a play or two, with Sperry's wife reading the heroine, and the rest of us taking other parts. She has a lovely voice, has Mrs. Sperry. But it was all stale and unprofitable, after the Wells affair. With Herbert on a lecture tour on spirit realism, and Mrs. Dane at a sanatorium for the winter, we have now given it up, and my wife and I spend our Monday evenings at home.

After dinner I read, or, as lately, I have been making this record of the Wells case from our notes. My wife is still fond of the phonograph, and even now, as I make this last entry and complete my narrative, she is waiting for me to change the record. I will be frank. I hate the phonograph. I hope it will be destroyed, or stolen. I am thinking very seriously of having it stolen.

"Horace," says my wife, "whatever would we do without the phonograph? I wish you would put it in the burglar-insurance policy. I am always afraid it will be stolen."

Even here, you see! Truly thoughts are things.

Made in the USA
Coppell, TX
16 August 2021

60545772R00056